THE SILVER BOX

ALSO BY MARGI PREUS
PUBLISHED BY THE UNIVERSITY OF MINNESOTA PRESS

Enchantment Lake: A Northwoods Mystery

The Clue in the Trees: An Enchantment Lake Mystery

THE
SILVER
BOX

AN
ENCHANTMENT LAKE
MYSTERY

MARGI PREUS

UNIVERSITY OF MINNESOTA PRESS

Minneapolis · London

Published by the University of Minnesota Press
111 Third Avenue South, Suite 290
Minneapolis, MN 55401-2520
http://www.upress.umn.edu

Library of Congress Cataloging-in-Publication Data
Preus, Margi, author.
The silver box : an Enchantment Lake mystery / Margi Preus.
Minneapolis : University of Minnesota Press, [2020]
Identifiers: LCCN 2020023679 (print) | ISBN 978-1-5179-0968-0 (hardcover) |
    ISBN 978-1-5179-0969-7 (paperback)
Subjects: CYAC: Mystery and detective stories. | Missing persons—Fiction. |
    Lakes—Fiction. | Great-aunts—Fiction. | Minnesota—Fiction.
Classification: LCC PZ7.P92434 Sil 2020 (print) | DDC [Fic]—dc23
LC record available at https://lccn.loc.gov/2020023679

Printed in the United States of America on acid-free paper

The University of Minnesota is an equal-opportunity educator and employer.

25 24 23 22 21 20   10 9 8 7 6 5 4 3 2 1

CONTENTS

I
THE WOLF

EVEN BEFORE SHE LIFTED HER HEAD from the pillow, Francie remembered: everything about her life had changed. Or was about to. Or had the potential to. Rising on one elbow, she noticed that even the light was different. No longer the egg-yolk yellow of fall, this morning's light was the pale, skim milk color of winter.

It had snowed—and was still snowing, falling from the sky in fat, sugarcoated flakes.

"I must be hungry," she mumbled, flinging off the blankets and mincing barefoot across the cold cabin floor. Past the slumbering bodies in their sleeping bags—her older brother Theo on the floor, her friend Jay on the couch, and Raven up in the loft. Past the cold fireplace filled with ashes. Past the empty wood box. Past the coffee table upon which sat—her heart gave a thump—the box.

It wasn't just the light or the snow that had changed, it was *that*: a small, intricately engraved silver box that she believed had once belonged to her mother. A box she had thought about for most of her seventeen years. Now it belonged to her. And it might, just might, bring her mother back to her.

A little shiver of anticipation ran through her, although perhaps it was just plain cold, she thought, as she hopped from one bare foot to the other. Standing on one foot, she picked up the box, which was not much bigger than a one-pound block of butter, and ran her fingers over its surface. The engraved designs of trees gave the impression of a kind of fairy-tale forest. An impenetrable forest, it seemed to Francie, as there was no discernible way to open the box! Could it even be considered a box if it didn't open? Still, it was so beautiful—in a gloomy sort of way. Though the trees gleamed silver, the dark tarnish along the edges gave the forest a foreboding look. *Beware of entering!* it seemed to say, and Francie had to admit: she was afraid.

She set the box down on the coffee table and, purposely averting her eyes from it, told herself, *A fire first, then I'll study the box more closely.*

She stuffed her feet into Theo's boots. (All she had brought to the cabin were her sneakers—who would have thought it would snow on Thanksgiving weekend?) She threw on Theo's parka, too, and crept outside, trying not to wake the others.

First she made a quick, shivery visit to the outhouse and then headed for the woodpile. With her head down to keep the falling snow out of her eyes, she couldn't help noticing that many creatures had already been up and about. There were the widely spaced hop marks of a rabbit and there, the little stitch marks of mice. And then something that made her stop and stare: big, human footprints punched into the snow. She could still make out the pattern of the tread of boot soles, so they must be fairly recent.

Glancing behind her at the cabin, she wondered if one of her friends or her brother had been out already, then gone back to sleep. Without bringing in any wood to stoke up the fire?

But the soft depressions in the snow didn't lead to the outhouse or to the woodpile or even down to the lake, as she would have expected. Instead, they led back into the woods that, as far as Francie knew, stretched all the way to Canada. Who could it be? All the cabins were shuttered and closed up—not a soul to be seen. Not a dock out. All boats off the lake. And definitely no cars: there was no road on this side of the lake.

She pulled Theo's jacket snug and stood for a moment staring at the lake—or where she knew the lake to be. A dark line of trees was visible along the near shore, but everything beyond dissolved into a misty whiteness.

She blinked away the snowflakes on her eyelashes, turned, and started to follow the tracks. As snow settled into the footprints ahead of her, they slumped into ill-defined round circles, simple holes punched in the snow that could have been made by anything—a deer, a bear, or, she thought at nearly the same time as she saw it standing just at the edge of the forest, a wolf.

He was huge and noble, with his thick coat of silver-gray fur and watchful yellow eyes, the royalty of this kingdom, the way the lion is king of the Serengeti. Or maybe, Francie thought, this wolf was the *queen*! And queenly she looked, literally shimmering, as if silver threads were woven into her coat. The wolf's yellow eyes flamed with something that set Francie's heart racing, something ancient and wise yet utterly wild. In some deep place inside her, Francie felt her own wild nature flutter to life.

Then the wolf shook itself, casting off a glittering shower of snow, and disappeared as if in a magician's cloud of smoke.

Francie staggered back toward the cabin, the footprints forgotten, as if she'd fallen under a spell. The crack of a rifle shattered the stillness, jolting Francie straight out of her enchantment, and sent her racing for the cabin.

2

THE PUZZLE BOX

FRANCIE PLUNGED INSIDE, closed the door, and leaned her back against it, breathing hard.

The cabin was the image of tranquility and normality. A fire crackling in the fireplace. Jay rolling up his sleeping bag. Theo bustling around the kitchen. Raven running a comb through her long hair.

"Is there some kind of hunting going on?" Francie gasped.

"We heard that gunshot, too," Jay said.

"It's deer hunting season," Raven said. "You should be careful out there. I wouldn't go out in the woods without wearing blaze orange right now."

"So it isn't wolf season?" Francie asked.

"There is no wolf season," Jay said. "There was a wolf hunt some years ago. People keep trying to bring it back, though."

"So nobody's hunting wolves right now?" Francie asked. She kicked off her boots and slid out of her jacket.

"Well, not legally," Raven said.

"Why all these questions about wolves?" Theo called from the kitchen.

"I saw one," Francie said.

"Cool!" Raven exclaimed.

"Scary!" Jay said.

"Well, anyway, it's good you're back," Theo said, walking out of the kitchen carrying four steaming mugs on a tray. "We've got to get going. You need to get back to your apartment in town—you've got school on Monday."

"I'm aware," Francie said.

"And I have a flight to catch this afternoon."

"What?" Francie said. "Theo! Where are you—"

"We all have to get back to school!" Jay said. "Trig test on Monday."

"But how?" Raven asked. "We don't have a boat, remember?"

"Somebody call Sandy and ask if he'll come get us," Theo said.

"I don't have a phone," Raven said, plopping down on the couch.

"My phone is dead," said Jay who plunked himself into an easy chair.

"And mine is on the bottom of the lake," Francie said. "Remember? It was in my hand when I fell through the ice. I must have dropped it—silly me."

Theo set the tray down on the coffee table and gave Francie a little hug. "I'll see if I can get a signal," he said, starting toward the kitchen. "I have a hard time getting service out here."

"Theo," Francie said, "where are you going?"

"To the kitchen," he answered over his shoulder.

"That's not what I mean!"

Even though Theo, at twenty-two, was five years older than Francie, in some ways he had not outgrown his annoying ways. Or else Francie had not outgrown being annoyed by him.

Raven took a mug from the tray while Jay tapped the silver box with his index finger. He looked up at Francie and said, "We were looking at this earlier, but we can't figure it out."

Francie felt a flash of irritation that they had been examining the box without her, but she swallowed it down and nudged Raven over to sit next to her on the couch.

"Another mystery already!" Raven beamed. "Isn't that cool?"

Francie didn't know how she felt about sharing this mystery with anyone else. This was *her* mystery, one she'd carried secretly in her heart all of her seventeen years, or, well, about thirteen years—ever since her mother had disappeared when she was just a tot. Where had her mother gone, and why? What did this box have to do with it, if anything? Francie had always believed the box was at the heart of it. And why that was so was also a mystery.

Theo stood in the doorway, his phone pressed to his ear. "Have some cocoa while it's still hot," he coaxed her gently. His face was tender. *We're all in this together now*, it seemed to say. *You don't have to go alone into the dark recesses of your memory. We all love and care about you.*

Francie knew how true this was. Raven and Jay and Theo had no doubt saved her life just a few days earlier. But none of them could understand how much she both longed to know yet also feared to know what secrets the box might hold.

But now, she thought, she looked at it with new eyes: wild, fierce, powerful—her wolf eyes. *Whatever is to be learned, I can handle it. I want to know.*

"I can tell this box is important to you," Jay said, lightly touching it with the tip of one finger. "But why?"

Theo looked at his phone, then put it in his pocket. "No answer," he said. "As for the box's significance, we can tell you, but this is very private information. And you can't tell anyone. For the safety of everyone."

Raven and Jay leaned forward, and Francie took a mug of cocoa, which she sipped while Theo told what he knew about their mother. "Our mother worked for the CIA," he began.

Even though Francie had learned that mind-blowing piece of information from Theo already, hearing it again sent a jolt through her. Rather than helping to solve the mystery, it just compounded it.

Raven and Jay stared at Theo, their mouths hanging open like cartoon stereotypes. Then Jay let out a low whistle. "Wow. Like, she was a spy?"

"We don't know. But after she had us kids she went into something she thought was safer—antiquities recovery. When a very rare and valuable item disappeared under her watch, she came under suspicion by her department."

"Because they thought she'd stolen it?" Raven said.

"Yeah," Theo explained.

"Did she?" Raven asked.

"Probably, but I think she had a reason. A good reason."

"But why didn't she turn the item over to the authorities?"

"We don't know," Theo said. "It's one of many things we have to figure out," Theo went on. "When I say *we*, I mean Frenchy and me. If you want to be involved, we trust you, but I have to tell you, it could be dangerous. Whatever happened—whoever she got mixed up with—well, it was serious enough that she had to go underground. She faked her own death and disappeared."

Raven and Jay had been staring at him open-mouthed as he delivered this speech. When he finished, Raven shook herself as if experiencing a little ripple of excitement. "Of course we're in, right, Jay?" she asked.

Jay gave a vigorous nod and said, "Well, yeah!"

Theo turned to his sister. Francie was feeling relieved: the story of her mother had long been a burden, having to tell everyone that her mother was dead while suspecting that she was not. So it was a relief not to pretend about that anymore. At least with her two best friends. Still, it had been her secret, and now it was not, and she didn't know how she felt about that.

"So this must be it, right? The valuable antiquity?" Raven asked, holding up the box.

"It's either the box or what's inside," Theo said. "At least, I'm pretty sure."

"But there isn't any way to get inside!" Raven exclaimed.

"It must be a puzzle box," Jay said.

"That's a thing?" Francie asked, taking a sip of hot chocolate.

"Yeah," Jay said. "You know—like it has a secret way of opening. You slide a little panel and press a spring and it pops open—that kind of thing. My dad gave me one years ago. I kept my baby teeth in it."

"Ew," Raven said.

"It was much easier than this one. But, hey! My dad knows a guy who's kind of an expert on puzzle boxes!"

"Right now the box is just between the four of us. Nobody else," Theo said. "Sorry."

Jay shrugged, and Theo walked to the window and stood there with the phone pressed to his ear. Francie glanced at him, then beyond him at the snow still pouring down.

"But I don't see how the box is going to help you find your mom," Raven said.

"I don't either, but I've always believed that it would. I guess that's pretty irrational," Francie said.

Theo pocketed his phone and turned back to them. "Still nobody."

"Maybe your flight will be canceled," Francie said hopefully.

"Haven't got any updates, so I assume it's going."

"Where are you going, and why now? Of all times!" She gestured to the box.

"Frenchy," Theo said, ignoring her question as he so often did, "you said you remember playing with this box when you were younger. Can you remember anything else about it?"

Francie closed her eyes, willing a memory to come, of the box, of how it opened. She felt it starting at the back of her mind, a memory from earliest childhood; she could almost hear the rustle of clothing, catch the scent of her mother . . . but the memory blurred and faded, as it always did when she tried to recall those early times.

A knock at the door made them all jump. Francie flinched, and she remembered the footprints outside, the footprints she had followed not long before and had forgotten to mention.

Theo leaned forward and whispered, "Not a word of this to anyone—no matter who it is." Then he whisked the box away into the bedroom while Francie got up to open the door.

It was Sandy from the resort across the lake. He stood on the stoop, wearing a little extra cap of snow on top of his stocking hat. His face was flushed from cold or exertion, or maybe he was blushing, something he seemed to do a lot around Francie.

"Hey, Frenchy," Sandy said. "I thought I should maybe check in on you."

Francie relaxed. It was not some weird, rifle-toting wolf hunter. Just Sandy.

"I thought you might need a ride. I mean, all you guys," Sandy added, peeking in at the others. "I came over in the boat," he added unnecessarily, considering there was no other way he could have gotten there.

"Thanks for coming over here in a snowstorm, Sandy," Francie said.

"Aw," Sandy said. "It's not a storm—it's only snow! And it's letting up. See?"

Everyone turned to look out the window. As if on Sandy's command, a crack opened in the roiling gray clouds and sunlight streamed down, creating what looked like a pool of molten gold on the open water.

"It looks like the legendary treasure of Enchantment Lake," Raven said.

Funny, Francie had been thinking the same thing.

"Most of the ice went out with the wind last night," Sandy went on, "so it wasn't too bad getting over here. I needed to get the boat out of there because there were these weird dudes pestering my mom to rent a boat. Said they wanted to go fishing!"

Once again the footprints reappeared in Francie's memory. Could it have been one of those guys? But, no, they'd have needed a boat to get over here, and Sandy had the boat. So who?

"Well, it'd be great to get a ride," Jay said. "I need to get home before my parents kill me. Plus, we have a trig test on Monday."

"Oh yeah," Raven said, not too happily.

"I guess we all need a ride," Theo said, appearing in the bedroom doorway.

Raven and Jay began stuffing their things in their backpacks, and Francie went in the bedroom to get her things, too.

"Theo, you can't go now!" Francie confronted her brother. "Where are you even going?"

"I'm sorry!" Theo said, "I don't want to, but somebody has to help Granddad after his surgery."

"You're going to New York? Can't he just hire somebody to take care of him? I thought you and I were finally going to try to find Mom!"

"Look," Theo said, "I'll just be gone for a few days." He stuffed a pair of jeans in his pack, then a sweater. "Just to make sure he's okay. After that I'll find someone to come in if he needs it. Just don't do *anything* until I come back."

Francie grabbed the socks he'd picked up out of his hand. "These are mine!"

"Oh," Theo said. "Sorry."

"Why can't I come, too?" she whined.

"And mess up your senior year in high school? Isn't your apartment, your living expenses—isn't that all contingent on you being in school, getting good grades, et cetera?" Theo said.

Francie groaned. It was true. Granddad had made it clear that he would only support her living here—close to the lake she loved and close to her great-aunts, at least before they'd gone south for a few months—if she stayed in school and kept up her grades.

"I never get to go anywhere. Why do you get all the fun?" Francie pouted.

"Fun?" Theo looked skeptical. "Taking care of Granddad?"

"Well, at least you'll be somewhere else," Francie said. "Somewhere exciting."

"You haven't had enough excitement here? Let's see, in the past few days . . . ," Theo began to enumerate, ". . . you went to the cabin by yourself, fell through the ice and nearly froze to death, were trapped in an underground tunnel and almost killed by a butcher knife–wielding assailant. That was just the past two days. Today you woke to a snowstorm, encountered a wolf . . . What kind of excitement were you longing for?"

"I just don't want to be left out!" Francie cried. "You'll be in New York and I'll be stuck in second-hour English examining my split ends!" She held up the ends of her hair to demonstrate.

"Pretty sure you'll find a way not to be left out, French," Theo said as he reached for the silver box.

"Wait!" Francie lunged at the box, but Theo jerked it away. "Theo, you can't—you can't! You don't understand how long I've looked for it!" Francie argued.

"Both it and you will be safer if it goes with me," Theo said.

"Theo, listen," Francie implored her brother. "I've always thought that if I got the box, I'd somehow get Mom back, too. You knew her long enough to remember her. You can probably picture her face. I can't—this is the only thing I've ever had of hers! You can't take her away from me again."

Theo looked at her, his dark eyes like melting chocolate. Although he was frustrating, in only the way a brother can be, still Francie had to admit, he had his tender side. He handed her the sweater-wrapped bundle. "You've always known how to get your own way," he said, zipping shut his backpack. "Don't let anybody know you have it, okay? Other than Raven and Jay, since they know about it already. Do not show it to anybody—anybody—else. Got that? And do not lose it!"

"Of course I'm not gonna lose it!" Francie said. "But how am I supposed to find out anything if I can't show it to anyone?"

"Frenchy," Theo said gently, "if there's anyone who can solve this mystery, it's you. You know more than anyone."

"How can you say that?" Francie angrily stuffed her clothes into her duffle bag. "Why doesn't anybody ever tell me anything, like where Mom went? Or why? Why do you keep it from me?" She stopped for a moment to settle the box carefully on top of her clothes in her backpack.

Theo gently laid his big warm hand on hers. "Frenchy—you're the one who knows," he said. "You were there."

"I was where?" Francie stared at him. "What are you saying?"

"When mom disappeared. You were there."

"You guys ready to go?" Sandy knocked on the bedroom door. "I gotta get back. My mom didn't know I came over here," he said, his voice cracking with anxiety. "I'm sure she's worried about me."

"Okay, we're coming," Theo said.

"Theo!" Francie yelped. "Tell me what you mean!"

"And to be honest, I'm worried about her," Sandy went on, talking through the door. "There was something strange about those guys. One guy with a funny accent. The other one didn't talk. All brand-new clothes—like they'd just bought everything new at Fleet Farm. Mom told them to come back when the lake was frozen and go ice fishing."

Francie and Theo came out of the bedroom to see that Sandy had doused the fire and pulled the shades. Raven and Jay were standing by the door, bundled up in their winter wear, looking already cold. Or perhaps afraid.

They all left the cabin, and Raven, Jay, and Sandy started for the boat. Francie hung back with Theo while he locked the door.

"Listen, Theo," Francie said. "You have to tell me what you meant when you said I had been there. I had been where?"

"You were here when Mom disappeared." He handed her the cabin keys and said, "Come on, the others are waiting."

Francie didn't move.

"Here?" Francie said incredulously. "Here at the cabin?"

"In the woods back there." Theo nodded toward the forest.

Where everything happens, Francie thought as she plodded through the deep snow behind her brother. At least an awful lot of things had happened there just in the few months she'd lived in this part of the world.

"It was in the summer," Theo said, talking to her over his shoulder. "We were here. Mom, you, me, the aunts. Not Dad—he was traveling. Mom went to pick blueberries. She wanted to go alone, but you begged to go along and I didn't want to baby-sit you. You cried and fussed, and I probably whined and complained and finally Mom just took you."

A flash of something—*the scent of damp leaves and earth; a sky the almost purple of blueberries.* "And then . . . ?" Francie asked. She grabbed Theo's arm, stopping him.

"Then she disappeared," he said.

"Just . . . disappeared," Francie repeated.

"Yes." He turned and faced her.

"But I didn't?"

"Well, actually you did, too."

"Huh? I disappeared, too?"

"For a couple of days."

Francie was stunned into speechlessness. She stared down at the lake where Sandy was handing life jackets to Raven and Jay, then said, "What happened? Was I with Mom? Was I wandering out in the woods? *What?*"

"Nobody knows," Theo said.

"But where had I been?" Francie pleaded with him. "Tell me something!"

"We searched the blueberry patch and all over back there, and then you showed up two days later, perfectly sound. I found you tugging on the screen door trying to open it, just like any ordinary day."

Blueberry patch . . . Francie tried to picture it. When was the last time she'd been there? This past summer she'd gone strawberry picking with her great-aunts, until Aunt Astrid announced she was going to hunt for diamonds instead. And before this summer there had been a lot of years when she hadn't gone to the cabin at all. Granddad made sure of that.

Now when she tried to call up the picture of the place, what came instead were black-and-white illustrations from a children's book: a bear cub and a little girl in overalls, both eating blueberries from the same patch . . .

Sandy shouted from the lake. "Are you coming?" He held on to the boat while the others clambered into it.

"We should go," Theo said to Francie. "We can talk more about this in the car on the way to the airport."

He started down the stairs and Francie stumbled after, trying to walk in the footprints punched into the snow by the others. "How did I get home? Where had I been?"

"I don't know!" an exasperated Theo said as they reached the boat. He threw his bag over the side. "Come on, get in." He held out his hand to help her, but she shook her head.

"No, I'm going to stay."

"Stay? No!"

"Come on!" Raven and Jay yelled from their seats in the boat. "Hurry up!"

"There's something I need to do," Francie said.

"Do it later," Theo said. "We have a ride now."

Francie turned to Sandy. "I'm sorry, Sandy. Would you come back for me tomorrow?"

"You're serious!" Raven cried.

"Don't be difficult," Theo said, stepping into the boat. "I've got a plane to catch and no extra time for your tantrums. And you need to give me a ride to the airport."

"I am not having a tantrum, and Jay will give you a ride to the airport. Right, Jay?"

"Sure," Jay said. "No problem!"

Francie turned to Sandy and said, "I'd really appreciate it if you can come back for me tomorrow."

"You bet," he said as he started to shove the boat off the beach.

"Wait!" Raven called. She climbed back out of the boat, missing the shore by an inch and getting her feet wet in the process.

"What are you doing?" Francie said. "You can go with the others. I'll be fine."

"I'm staying, and that's that." Raven hopped onto dry land.

Theo leaned over the boat and handed Raven his phone. "Here," he said. "One of you has to at least have a phone. Give it to Francie. I'll get a new one."

Jay waved goodbye, and Theo threw up his hands and plunked himself down on a seat, while Sandy expertly turned the boat around and aimed it toward the far shore. The motor roared as the boat sped away.

3

SNOWSHOEING

"So, what's up?" Raven said, once they were back in the cabin and she had stripped off her wet boots.

"Sorry about you getting wet like that," Francie called from the bedroom, where she was going through her aunts' dresser drawers. "I know how cold that water is."

"Yeah, I know you do," Raven said, peeling a wet sock from her foot. "It's a wonder you're alive. What did Nels say when you told him?"

Nels! Francie thought with a start. Her mind flashed on his tousled, sun-bleached hair. His incandescent smile. He'd probably been calling and calling wondering why she didn't answer. Not knowing her phone was on the bottom of the lake. Not knowing she'd fallen through the ice, or that she'd almost drowned, or that she'd almost been killed by a butcher knife–wielding assailant. There was so much stuff he didn't know: it was like an entire book of her life had gone by without him in it.

She emerged from the bedroom with a balled-up pair of wool

socks, a pair of long johns, and some fairly ancient but warm-looking woolen trousers, all of which she deposited in Raven's lap. "I guess he doesn't know," she said.

"He's your boyfriend! Shouldn't you call him?"

"Sure," Francie said, heading back to the closet, this time looking for a pair of boots for herself, now that Theo's were on his feet—and gone.

"I'm using Theo's phone to call my mom right now," Raven said. "I'll tell her I'm spending another night with you—back tomorrow."

"Good idea," Francie called from the closet. The farther into the closet she went, the further thoughts of Nels receded. She could hear Raven's voice, talking to her mom. Nels could wait, Francie decided, until she had more time.

"What's up, anyway?" Raven stood in the closet doorway. "Why did you suddenly decide you had to stay?"

"Why did you decide to stay with me?" Francie asked.

"Because you're about to do something crazy, and I don't think you should do it alone," Raven said.

"Me? Crazy?" Francie laughed. "I just want to go find the blueberry patch."

"No, that's not crazy!" Raven said. "Blueberry picking in a November snowstorm—perfectly normal!"

"I just want to go find the blueberry patch I used to go to when I was a kid."

"Because . . . ?"

"It has to do with Mom."

"It'll be hard to find blueberry bushes this time of year. Especially when everything is covered with snow."

Francie had already thought about that and knew it was true. She didn't mention to Raven that she hadn't been to that blueberry patch since she was a toddler. If Raven knew that, she would know for sure Francie was crazy. Maybe she already did.

In the far reaches of the closet she hit pay dirt: winter boots.

"I'm just going to go out and see if I can find it," Francie said, her voice muffled as she receded farther into the closet, tossing out boots, a down jacket, some wool socks, everything suffused with the cinnamon roll and wood-smoke scent of her aunties. It seemed odd to be here at their cabin without them. "You don't have to come along. Stay here by the fire."

"What fire?" Raven laughed.

"The one you're going to make," Francie said. "So the cabin is nice and toasty when I get back."

"Nope," Raven said. "If you're going, I'm going."

"What about your wet boots?"

"Seems like you're finding plenty of auntie clothing in there. See if you can locate a pair of boots, size eight."

"You're sure?" Francie said.

"I'm going to pack some water, matches, and a headlamp," Raven said, heading for the kitchen. "Plus some turkey sandwiches from yesterday's leftovers."

"We're not going to be gone that long!" Francie called after her.

"We did not have breakfast!" Raven shouted back.

"Oh yeah," Francie said, all of a sudden realizing her stomach felt as empty as a northern Minnesota town in the middle of a January night. If the aunties had been here, she thought, there'd be bacon and eggs right now. And cinnamon rolls, of course. "Eureka!" she yelped. "Look what I found!" She emerged from the closet with two pairs of old wooden snowshoes.

"Promise me you won't let me freeze to death," Francie said, once she and Raven were outside. Francie was bundled up as if she were a bubble-wrapped porcelain vase about to be shipped to the other side of the world.

"You won't freeze," Raven said. "You just don't want to get too hot."

Francie laughed. "Too hot—ha ha!"

"You don't want to sweat. You don't want a soggy down jacket in this temperature. You want to be able to peel off layers."

"There is no way I am going peel off anything!" Francie shouted after Raven who had started off, following the path that led into the woods behind the cabin.

"I predict a striptease!" Raven called back, laughing. "Which way?"

Francie pointed at a kind of cleared path that continued into the forest. Raven broke trail with Francie following. It was awkward at first, walking like Bigfoot, and she had to stop a couple of times to adjust the bindings. After a while she got the hang of it, and then it was just the stillness and silence, broken only by their puffing breaths and the crunch of the snow under their snowshoes.

After her initial fear of freezing to death, and as she felt her body warm, and that warmth spread to her feet and hands and even to her face, she began to notice the beauty of the forest around her: the bright, clean world of white, the snow-laden trees, and the glittering confetti kicked up by Raven's snowshoes. She also noticed she was too warm.

Francie stopped and slipped off her backpack in order to peel off her top layer. "How is this possible?" she mumbled.

"You're working," Raven said. "Burning some calories."

"That's for sure." Francie panted.

The two of them stood for a moment while Francie's heart rate and breathing calmed down. In the quiet, they listened to the solemn tapping of a woodpecker, and a raven auditioning as if for voice-over work. The disapproving gurgle. Giddy falsetto. Death rattle. Beyond that, the silence seemed to stretch forever, as if the rest of the world had fallen away.

"You know that story *Blueberries for Sal?*" Francie said.

"Is that the one where the little white girl goes blueberry picking with her Mom and they get separated? Meantime, mama and baby bear are also grazing blueberries, and they also get separated. Little white girl almost goes home with mama bear, and baby bear almost goes home with white girl's mama."

"Her name is *Sal*, Raven, not *Little White Girl*."

Raven laughed. "Well, if it were a little Ojibwe girl, everyone would say Little Native Girl or Little Indian Girl, admit it."

"You're probably right."

After a drink of water, they moved on, along a path through the forest, and eventually into an area of sort of scruffy-looking jack pines.

"This is where your blueberries are," Raven said, turning a circle.

"How do you know?" Francie asked.

"You think I've never picked blueberries?" Raven said, throwing her arms out. "This would be just the kind of place I'd look. There was a forest fire here not too many years ago."

"How do you know that?"

"Jack pines. Not too tall. They're the first to grow after a fire. Their cones don't open except in the superheat of fire. And that kind of soil that you find in a burned area—whatever it is— blueberries like it. And some sunlight. So, is this it, do you think?" Raven asked, clomping around in a circle to take a look.

Francie could almost smell the summertime scent of moss and pine needles, of hummocky ground covered in low-growing bushes laden with dark, purplish blueberries. The sound of the first berry hitting the bottom of the pail—just like in the story—

she could hear it in her memory, *Plink!* and the second one, *Plunk!*

Just like little Sal in the story, Francie had been unable to stop eating them. The taste was purple: it tasted like summer, like sunshine, like piney woods and bare feet and straw hats.

"So . . . ?" Raven said. "See what you needed to see? Should we head back?"

"This is not where the journey ended," Francie murmured. She and her mother had not filled their buckets with berries and hiked home that day. She had snatched up only a few handfuls and then her mother had urged her along. "Come on, Franny," she had said.

Franny, her mother had called her. How long had it been since she'd remembered that? Funny to remember it now. She'd had so many names in her life: Francesca, Francie, Frenchy, French-Fry . . . and now she remembered the name that only her mother had used: Franny. Which one was her real name? Which was the real her?

"Come on, Franny," her mother had said, and they had trundled on. Francie almost had to run to try to keep up with her mother. Branches and brambles scratched her arms. Her mother had picked her up and to quiet her crying told her a story.

"*Far far away in a lake lies an island*," her mother had said, and now Francie murmured it aloud as she walked toward a stand of tall pines.

"What did you say?" Raven said, following. "And are you sure it's a good idea to go much farther?"

Among the pines, Francie's memory sharpened. She remembered the light filtering through the boughs, and clinging to her mother, who was speaking softly, "*On that island is a church . . . .*" Where were they going? Why was her mother hurrying so? Was someone chasing them?

"*In the church is a well . . . .*"

Now, the seventeen-year-old Francie looked over her shoulder, as if looking for her four-year-old self. Or perhaps she was looking to see if someone had been following them all those long years ago. If there had been anyone then, she hadn't known. Or she didn't remember.

Today, Francie led the way, following her instinct. It had been wet, she remembered. "*In that well swims a duck,*" her mother had said as she sloshed through marshes and bogs, holding Francie above the water. Even so, Francie's feet had gotten wet.

Now she and Raven floated above the frozen marsh on snowshoes, tromping among broken cattails. She trudged toward a birch grove in the distance. "*In the duck there is an egg . . . .*"

"Do you know where you are going?" Raven asked.

"Sort of," Francie said. "I don't know why, but, yes, I sort of do."

"*Sort of* is not a confidence-building answer," Raven said. "I mean, if we're lost, it's okay. If we turn around now, we can follow our tracks back to the cabin. But we should do it soon. It gets dark early, you know."

"Just a little farther." Francie was like a dog with its nose to the ground, following a trail. She was a mole, scurrying along a well-worn path. She was a fish, swimming with an unseen school of fish, purposefully driven forward by—what? She couldn't say.

Was there something familiar about that big fir tree with its branches spread so wide that an entire kindergarten class could picnic under it? These birches—had she walked through a grove like this thirteen years ago? The way the land sloped—she imagined it blooming with daisies. Here is where the trail gave out and Francie began to doubt.

"*In the egg . . . in the egg . . . .*" What was in the egg?

"Are we lost?" Raven said.

"No." Francie desperately wanted to believe that. "We're looking for something. That is not the same as being lost."

"Is *that* what we're looking for?" Raven said, pointing through the trees.

Francie craned her neck, squinted, and then saw it: a building. A kind of cabin or maybe more of a shack, its siding so weathered as to be almost camouflaged among the browns and grays of the winter trees.

As the two friends moved toward it, its outline sharpened: a droopy roof with shingles missing, windows boarded up, the front step listing to one side, and saplings sprung up all over in the yard.

"Sneezy, Grumpy, Goofy, Snotty, Doofus, Goofus, and Ridiculous," Raven said.

"What are you talking about?" Francie mumbled.

"I bet that's who lives here," Raven explained. "We're going to go in there, and there will be seven little beds, seven little chairs around the table, seven little dirty bowls in the sink. Or, if not the seven dwarves, maybe it's full of zombies. Should we go inside? You first."

Francie did not need to go inside to know what it was like: a rustic table made of wide pine planks, rough benches constructed of half-logs, a pine floor, a woodstove in one corner.

"I've been here before," she said.

4

THE RAMSHACKLE CABIN

"Well," Raven said, "I suppose that could happen—why not? It's not that far from your aunts' cabin, right?"

"Yes," Francie said uncertainly. When had she been here? How? With whom? What had transpired? None of those answers would come.

"Do you think it's open?" Raven said. "Come on, let's see." They took their snowshoes off and leaned them against a tree. Then Raven tugged on Francie's arm as they walked to the door.

The padlock on the door was not locked, and Raven opened the door. The smell of Christmas rushed out.

Except for the thin light that entered from the open door, the inside of the cabin was dark, all its windows boarded over.

"What's crunching under our feet?" Francie asked as they walked inside.

Raven pulled a headlamp out of her pack and switched it on, aiming the light down at her feet. "Pine needles," she said. She swung the beam around the room and let out a laugh. "I guess

Sleepy, Slurpy, Dumpy, Grumpy, Argumentative, and the other dwarves are lumberjacks."

There were pine boughs and pine trees—tiny ones—everywhere, leaning up against the walls, on the couch, heaped on the chair, piled on the table.

"It really does look like the seven dwarves cut these, because they're so little!" Francie said, holding up a tiny tree. "Why?"

"All those outdoor pots and window boxes filled with what look like miniature Christmas trees? Where do you think they come from? Multiply the number of outdoor planters and window boxes in our wee town by the millions of window boxes and outdoor pots all over the country, all of which need to be filled with festive cheer—and you've got a big demand for tiny Christmas trees. They're not really tiny trees, they're the tops of big trees. They cut big trees down to take just their tops. How sad is that?"

"What a waste," Francie said. "But why bother putting trees inside a house?" She scratched her head through her knit cap. "I mean, they're trees, right? Like, they're used to being outside?"

"Unless you don't want anyone to see them?" Raven suggested. "I think you can get a permit to cut boughs and stuff, but I'm just gonna guess that these aren't legal. Otherwise, why hide them? With the deer hunters out in the woods now, someone might report it."

"Geez," Francie said. "Well, it's going to make it hard to look around. It's hard to see the forest for the trees, so to speak."

"What are you looking for?" Raven asked.

"Don't really know," Francie said.

Raven shone her headlamp around the space, revealing what was basically a one-room cabin, sparsely furnished, although it was hard to tell since there were trees everywhere. Aiming the light above their heads, she asked, "What's hanging from the rafters?"

"Herbs." Francie didn't even have to look to know. She closed her eyes for a moment and breathed in: a little of their scent could be discerned even through the potent smell of pine and fir. Or perhaps it was just in her memory. *Herbs and plants of all sorts hanging in bunches from the rafters, along with drying mushrooms and homemade venison sausages.*

There were no sausages or mushrooms now, but the smell came to her just the same: earthy, smoky, herby, spicy.

Francie pulled off a mitten, stepped up on a chair and reached over her head. She plucked something from one of the dried bunches of herbs, crushed the leaves in her fingers, held them to her nose, and inhaled. Years of frozen feeling began to thaw and emotions rushed through her like melting snow. *A woman . . . an old woman . . . who smelled like these herbs . . . her hair as white as snow . . . .*

The smell called to something deep in her memory. *Hushed voices, a sense of urgency . . . she felt maybe she was meant to hurry, to try to figure something out; if she figured it out, maybe everything would be okay, maybe everything would go back to the way it was.*

"Hey," Raven said. "Do you hear that?"

"Chainsaws?" Francie listened to the growl of machines.

Raven shook her head. "Snowmobiles. Let's get out of here."

"But—" Francie protested. She needed to find something more, something that would help her understand who had lived here. "I need to find *something!*"

The whining roar quickly became louder and more insistent.

"Come on," Raven said, grabbing Francie's arm. "Those snowmobiles are getting closer. What if it's hunters with rifles? Or the tree cutters? I don't want to be here either way!"

The girls moved toward the door, but not fast enough. The

snowmobiles rumbled to a stop outside, and men's voices rang sharp and clear as bells in the crystalline air.

Simultaneously, Francie and Raven dove for the only conceivable place to hide: the closet. They closed the closet door behind them just as the door to the cabin creaked open.

From inside the closet, Francie and Raven listened to boots shuffling along the floor and someone giving orders: "Take this pile first," and "No, not those," and "We've gotta get all these outta here." Cold air from the open door crept through the cracks in the closet, and with it the smell of damp wool and gasoline.

"We got some real nice ones this time," said a voice.

"Yep," came a grunted answer. Then the voices were muffled by the sounds of shuffling and scraping.

Francie and Raven hunched inside the dark closet, so close together that Francie felt Raven shivering. Francie was also shivering. Or possibly trembling.

Finally the men seemed to have finished their task. It seemed like they might leave, but then a youngish voice said, "Wasn't it an old witch who lived here?"

The voice was familiar to Francie. She was sure it belonged to someone she knew. Someone from school.

"A witch?" said someone else. "Only you would believe that. It was just some old lady."

"Yeah, she was a witch." The familiar voice again. "She did magic out here, grew herbs, made potions."

"Boys," an older man's deep voice boomed out, "you coulda learned a lot from that old lady. She was entirely self-sufficient. Hunted and grew her own food, cut her own firewood. She was a tough old broad. I'd like to see you two live for just a week out in the woods. You'd never survive without them goldarned phones you gotta be starin' at every two minutes."

"Hey! We just spent the whole cold day out in the woods," one of the boys protested.

"And that's the last you're going to say about it—to anyone. Got it? No bragging. Last thing we need is some conservation officer snooping around."

"Okay, yeah. But I'm just saying, maybe that old lady had a million bucks stashed in her mattress. I read about stuff like that happening."

"Where would she get a million bucks?" said someone else. "She didn't work. She lived out here on what she could hunt, fish, and grow. I'm sure she never had anything valuable. I mean, look at this place! It's a dump."

"That's exactly where you find someone has stashed a million bucks. Or, maybe not a million. A grand, though."

"That lady is still alive, you know, so if you found something, you'd be stealing."

Say her name, Francie thought. *Say her name.*

"She ain't living here no more, and she ain't ever getting back here to find her stash, either. Let me at least look around!"

Who belonged to that familiar whine? Francie wondered. By now she had to keep her teeth clamped together to prevent them from chattering. And the clink and clank of things being picked up and set down and of drawers being opened and shut had Francie and Raven clinging to each other. When boots stomped toward the closet, they clutched each other's hands. And when the doorknob rattled, Francie squeezed her eyes shut.

"Okay, that's enough," said a gruff-voiced man. "Come on! Let's hustle."

There was some grumbling and joshing and shuffling of feet, and then everyone was gone.

Francie and Raven waited until the snowmobiles started up

and roared away, and once the sound had faded, they crept out of the closet into the main room.

"Listen, Frenchy," Raven whispered, as if the men might be standing outside the door. "We really, really need to get going! Even if we leave this minute, it will be pitch-dark by the time we get back."

"Not yet!" Francie protested, heading to the cupboard. "I've waited thirteen years to get here. Now I need to at least find the lady's name! And where she might be." The cupboard turned up nothing but a couple of old cups and saucers. "She's still alive!" Francie said. "They said so!"

She moved to a chest of drawers. Nearly everything was empty—or had been emptied by others. Finally, in the bottom drawer, she found file folders.

"Come over here," Francie said, "and shine your light on this."

Raven held the light so Francie could look through the files. The ice-cold papers crinkled and rattled as Francie ran her mittens along them.

"It's gotta be dark by now!" Raven warned, hopping up and down either to vent frustration or to stay warm. "We've got to go . . ."

But Francie had found something. A file folder full of bills, all addressed to the same person. "Loretta Swift," Francie said out loud. "That's the old woman's name. This could be big, Raven. Important!"

"Awesome!" Raven charged past Francie to the door, calling over her shoulder, "Come on!"

Francie gathered up the file, stood up, and came toward the door where Raven stood, yanking hard on the handle.

"It's locked!" she cried. "They locked us in!"

5

STRANGE LODGINGS

"Thank goodness Theo gave me his phone." Francie extracted the phone from her pocket and stared despondently at the blank screen. "It's dead!"

"The cold drains the battery," Raven said. "There's probably not service out here anyway."

"Oh for frickin' frozen chicken fingers," Francie said. "Now what?"

"We have to find a way out." Raven turned a big circle, casting the beam of her headlamp all around the room. "Windows all boarded up."

"Just so you know," Francie said, "I'm not going up the chimney."

Raven moved to a window and slid it open. "Look at that!" she said. "The window opens!"

"How is that helpful?" Francie gestured to the piece of plywood covering the outside of the window.

"All we have to do is get the board off," Raven explained.

"How are we going to do that? It's nailed from the outside."

"Think about it," Raven said. "Maybe we can . . . I don't know . . ." Raven leaned back, stuck her foot through the window, and executed a karate-style kick at the plywood, nearly falling over in the process.

"Great form!" Francie said, laughing.

"It's not a laughing matter!" Raven said. "Help me!"

Francie tried kicking through the open window, and then Raven tried, and soon they had both fallen over and were on the floor, laughing. They laughed until they cried. And then they just cried.

Finally, wiping her tears, Francie got up and held out a hand. "Light-bulb moment," she said.

"Yeah?"

"We pull that table over, both of us lie down on it and get all four of our feet kicking at the same time."

"Eureka!" Raven said. "Let's try it."

Once the table was situated under the window, the two girls lay down on their backs and placed their feet through the open window on the piece of plywood.

"Ready, dance line?" Raven called out. "One, two, three, kick!"

It took several tries, but at last they heard the squeal of nails, the cracking of wood, and the groan of the board giving way. A few more kicks and the board was on the ground and Francie and Raven were dancing around the table, singing, "Freedom, Freedom, I can't move. Freedom, cut me loose!"

They lowered themselves out of the window and stood gulping the fresh air and staring out into the darkness.

"It's dark," Raven whispered. The beam of her headlamp illuminated the falling snow that danced around them.

"And snowing," Francie added, unnecessarily.

They turned to look at each other and said simultaneously, "What are we going to do?"

"There's a better-than-even chance that we'd get lost if we tried to get back to your cabin," Raven pointed out.

"How about following that snowmobile trail?" Francie offered.

"Do you know where it goes?" Raven asked.

Francie didn't. Neither did Raven.

"It could be miles and miles before we got anywhere," Raven said. "Also, I don't know how much battery life I've got left in this headlamp."

"So, what then?" Francie tried to keep the panic out of her voice.

"I think we should stay here."

"It's cold!" Francie shivered. She was damp, and standing in that cramped closet for so long had chilled her bone-deep. With twilight, the temperature had dropped, and the sharp cold pinched her cheeks and brought tears to her eyes.

"There's a woodstove in there," Raven pointed out. "And plenty of kindling in the form of the boughs and stuff those guys left behind. I bet there are some woodpiles around here, too." She shoved her hat down over her ears and stomped around the side of the cabin.

Francie followed, and while Raven pushed the snow off a pile of split wood, Francie peered out into the dim light. The shape of a wolf seemed to materialize out of the falling snow. Was that its outline she could see against the dark edge of the trees, or was she only imagining it?

"Hey!" Raven stood in front of her with an armload of wood. "Here." She shoved the load toward Francie, who took it and stumbled toward the still-open window. The wolf was gone—if there had ever been one.

They dumped several armloads of wood through the window, then climbed back inside and shut the window behind them.

Raven started making a fire while Francie stood with hunched shoulders staring at nothing.

"You need to move," Raven said, glancing over her shoulder. "Light that lamp." Raven aimed the headlamp beam on the table where there was a kerosene lamp, and Francie dutifully tromped over to it.

Francie fiddled clumsily with the wick of the kerosene lamp. What was wrong with her? Of course she knew how to light these things. After all, there was no electricity at her aunts' cabin. It was like her mind was full of falling snow.

"This is interesting," Raven said.

Francie turned, welcoming the distraction.

"The ashes are warm. There are even a few little embers burning in here."

"The tree cutters?" Francie suggested through chattering teeth. She tucked her hands under her armpits. She didn't feel cold, exactly. Just strange.

Raven stared at her for a moment and then said, "Hand me that bucket with kindling in it—maybe there's birch bark in there. Then take my headlamp and look around for some blankets."

Francie picked up a plastic five-gallon bucket containing kindling, a few shreds of yellowed newspapers, a bit of torn cardboard, and on the bottom a bit of birch bark. But when she picked it up, she saw it wasn't birch bark. It was a business card. The light was too dim to read it, so she stuck it in her pocket.

Raven got a fire going while Francie looked for blankets, which she found in a cedar chest that had miraculously not been looted.

As they sat in front of the crackling fire, chewing the sandwiches and granola bars they hadn't eaten earlier, Raven said, "I'll say one thing. Hanging out with you is never boring."

"I'm sorry about all this," Francie said. "But I'm glad you came along."

"Good thing, too," Raven said. "Or you'd probably be dead from hypothermia by now. Are you warming up okay?"

"Is that what was wrong with me just now?" Francie asked. "Hypothermia?"

"You were getting there," Raven said.

The cabin was now warm enough that Francie slid her jacket off, tucked it pillow-like under her head, then snuggled down under the blankets. She knew she should probably be worried. After all, she and Raven were far from anyone who could help them. No one knew where they were. Her phone was dead. There were strange tree poachers prowling about, and they were spending the night in a rickety shack that creaked and rattled in the wind. And yet, she really wasn't afraid.

Next to her, Raven's breathing was slow and steady. Francie sat up, reached for her backpack, and drew it toward her. She took out the box, unwrapped it from Theo's sweater, and examined it in the light of the fire. This puzzling thing, she thought, so beautiful and mysterious. The firelight flickered over the box, turning it from silver to a burnished red-gold, the color of warmth. She knew she was imagining it, but it almost felt warm to the touch.

Holding it in her hands, she had a sense of déjà vu, of having been here before, doing this exact thing. Everything seemed somehow comforting. The snow tapping quietly on the roof. The purring of the fire in the woodstove, the occasional snap of pine. A feeling that everything would turn out all right came over her.

They would be fine, Raven and Francie. The next day they would follow their tracks back, through bog and forest, aspen and birch groves, stands of pine and an area of jack pines where in the summertime blueberries grew, and finally to the old familiar cabin, where she had spent so many summers and which was now her home.

Home, she thought. She realized she'd never really felt that way about anywhere else. Yes, Enchantment Lake was home.

6

A PIPPI LONGSTOCKING LIFE

THE NEXT DAY had dawned bright and sunny, and Raven and Francie slogged their way back to the aunts' cabin through heavy, wet, melting snow. Sandy pulled up in his boat just as they got there, so they hopped in and rode across the brilliantly shining lake, doing a reprise of "Freedom, Freedom, I can't move. Freedom, cut me loose!" at the top of their lungs.

When Francie was little, her great-aunt Astrid had loved to read Pippi Longstocking stories to her. "By Astrid Lindgren," Aunt Astrid would always be sure to add before beginning to read about the redheaded Swedish girl with outlandish pigtails who lived all alone in a goofy house. Well, not exactly all alone: she lived with her horse and a monkey named Mr. Nilssen. Francie thought about Pippi every time she climbed the stairs of the house where she lived. It was a creaky, old place divided into four apartments, one of which was hers. Like Pippi, she lived all alone, although without pets of any kind. She knew it was unusual for a girl of her age to live alone, but she'd always been independent and was used to being away from family, since she had gone to a boarding school in New York for a lot of her life. Pippi, whose whole name was something like Pippilotta Delicatessa Windowshade Dandeliona Peppermint Longstocking, lived in a small town in Sweden. Francie (who, if you counted all her nicknames, had a name just as long—Francesca Francie Franny Frenchy French-Fry Frye) lived in the small town of Walpurgis, Minnesota.

A small business card fluttered to the floor when Francie opened the door.

She picked it up and read it in the dim light. "Louis Streife, Director of Development. Glentech." His phone number was circled and scrawled in ink were the words, "Please call me."

She had no intention of calling anyone, especially some man from some company she had never heard of. Although . . . . She suddenly remembered the card she'd found in Loretta's kindling bucket. She dug around in her jacket pocket and compared the two. Whoa. Same guy, same company. Was everybody in the area being contacted by the unfortunately named Louis Streife? *Gawd!* Francie thought. *Sounds like "loosestrife." Isn't that an invasive species?*

She locked the door behind her and tossed her keys on the small table inside the door. Although it had only been a few days, her apartment had that slightly surreal look of a place you know but isn't quite the way you remembered it. But there was her saggy couch. The slightly beat-up coffee table. The end table in the corner on which sat the small but prickly cactus her great-aunts had sent from Arizona; she'd finally put it in a corner so it wouldn't snag her clothes every time she passed by. Still, she smiled to see it, a little gift from her great-aunts. She assumed it had been Jeannette, the pricklier of the aunts, who had picked it out. And Astrid, Jeannette's sweet but scatterbrained sister, who had put a pink ribbon around the pot before sending it.

As she moved through her small apartment, Francie imagined Theo taking the lift to Granddad's penthouse suite on the twenty-fourth floor with its view of the city, its leather furniture and glass tabletops, plush carpets, and everything tasteful and expensive.

"Ha!" Francie laughed out loud. Her simple, slightly ramshackle apartment was a far cry from that. All her furnishings were from rummage sales or hand-me-downs from the cabin. But it was hers and she liked it.

Even after she had access to her trust fund, she might just keep all this junky furniture and this drafty apartment in this creaky old house. In the meantime, her grandfather provided her with living expenses—and that's exactly what she could do with it, she sometimes thought: stay alive.

She took the box out of her bag and set it on the kitchen table, still wrapped in its sweater. Too tired to do anything but go to bed, she didn't even have enough energy to try, one more time, to open it.

She should call Nels, she knew, and briefly imagined the pleasant rumble of his voice on the other end of the line. But it would be a long call, what with all she had experienced the past several days. She just didn't have the energy to recount all of that.

Francie felt as tired as an old, old person who had just attempted a triathlon. If only she didn't have to get up for school the next day she could lie down and sleep for days. Nels would have to wait for tomorrow, she thought, dragging herself into the bathroom to brush her teeth. She wouldn't have been surprised if her hair had gone completely white with the events of the past few days, but catching a glimpse of herself in the mirror she saw that there was still only the one white streak in her otherwise dark hair—an oddity she shared with her mother, or so she'd been told.

Looking down to spit out her toothpaste, she noticed something shiny under the vanity. A tube of lipstick. "Lipstick?" she said out loud. Never wore it. Maybe it was Raven's, she thought, setting it on the counter. She'd have to remember to ask.

Her bed was the most inviting thing she had seen in days, and she collapsed on it, still fully dressed, and closed her eyes. As she fell asleep, her mind was a jumble of this and that: the wolf, its yellow eyes, the drive to Walpurgis on the quiet roads past lakes in the process of freezing, the peculiar sound of pieces of ice clinking and clanking together like shattered china plates or broken crystal.

7

AT SCHOOL

"WINTER IS THE SEASON OF ABSENCE," Ms. Fitzroy was saying. The teacher, a sub, had a long, sad face and long, sad hair. She wore a black dress—or maybe it was a coat, hard to tell. Whatever it was, it made her appear to be leaving any minute to go to a funeral. But on she droned: "The absence of sun, warmth, light, scent, color."

The absence of Theo, Francie thought. The absence of the aunts, who had gone south for the winter. The absence of her parents. Both long gone. Her father dead in a car accident when she was seven. And her mother, gone for thirteen years.

After class, Ms. Hanover, the art teacher, approached Francie in the hallway and explained that she was going to be directing the winter musical.

"I heard you were very good as Antigone," Ms. Hanover said, breathlessly. "In the fall production," she added, as if Francie might not remember the play in which she played the lead role.

"I know all about you!" The art teacher's cheeks pinkened. "Acted in New York . . ."

"It's not like I was in any Broadway—"

"And on TV!" Ms. Hanover exclaimed.

"It wasn't—" Francie started to protest again. Her life in New York seemed so far away, when life had revolved around auditions and very few callbacks. Yes, she had been in a kids' TV show in which she played, of all things, a detective. Francie had been in only a few episodes before it was canceled.

"So what do you think? Will you be trying out for our winter show?" Ms. Hanover urged.

"Uh, no," Francie said. "Gotta buckle down on the homework."

"You're not even curious what it is?" Ms. Hanover stared at Francie with wide eyes and a kind of smirk, as if she were holding in a secret so great she might burst.

Francie didn't care what the show was. There was no way she was going to commit to rehearsals and show dates—not when she had the biggest mystery of her entire life to solve. But she also didn't want to hurt the new, young director's feelings, so she said, "What is it?"

"It's a new musical version of *Sleeping Beauty*! I thought you would be very good as—"

"The queen," Francie answered. She was always offered the part of the older woman, because everyone said she looked older than her seventeen years. The white streak in her otherwise dark hair no doubt added significantly to that effect.

"Why, yes!" Ms. Hanover exclaimed, pressing a flyer about upcoming auditions into Francie's hands. "But I'm sure you'd be good in any part!"

"Thanks, but I have to say no this time. I'm sure you'll find lots of talent, though. Gotta run or I'll be late for class!" Francie dashed off, leaving the hapless Ms. Hanover waving her flyers.

. . . . .

At lunch, Francie watched hungrily as Raven unwrapped the sandwich she'd brought from home.

"That looks so good!" Francie said.

"Homemade bread," Raven mumbled. "Leftover turkey, cran-berries, lettuce . . ."

"Did you make that?" Francie couldn't help but breathe in the heavenly fragrance of Raven's sandwich, in contrast to the gelatinous goo that oozed from the Styrofoam-like bun on her plate.

Raven shook her head. "Mom," she said. "She made the bread, too."

Francie stared down at her own questionable school lunch and tried not to feel envious that Raven had a mom who made her lunches. A mom who made homemade bread. A mom, period.

Jay arrived and slid onto the bench next to Francie. "So, I've been thinking about the box," he said, jerking Francie out of her food funk.

"Shh!" she said and began scooting herself and her tray to the far end of the table.

Her friends followed, pushing their lunches along with them.

"We're like outcasts," Jay said, "sitting down here like lepers."

"If we're going to talk about this stuff, we have to be lepers. Because this is totally secret, okay? You absolutely can't tell any-one," Francie said. "Remember what Theo said."

"Okay, but I've been thinking," Jay said. "It might not pan out to be anything, but we could take the box to that guy I was tell-ing you about—the puzzle box expert. He works at the county historical museum."

"What did I just say?" Francie said. "About not telling anyone? What about the Internet?"

"I already scoured it," Jay said.

"You did?"

"Of course he did." Raven casually peeled the crust off the other half of her sandwich.

"I'll eat that!" Francie said, snatching it away from her and stuffing it in her mouth. Then, with her mouth full of bread crust, she said, "Oh, by the way, Jay." She reached into her backpack for the file folder she'd taken from Loretta's cabin and handed it to him. "Can you do your wizardry and see if you can find out where this person is? She's elderly and may be incapacitated in some way, but I'm pretty sure she's still alive."

"That's all you know?" Jay asked.

"Pretty much," Francie was saying just as Phoebe appeared.

"All you know about what?" Phoebe asked, standing over them holding her lunch tray. Popular, blonde-haired Phoebe who had played Ismene, sister to Francie's Antigone, in the fall production. "So . . . ," Phoebe went on, with hardly a break, "tryouts are coming up! You guys are going to be involved again, right?" Phoebe was speaking mostly to Jay and Raven, both of whom had cemented themselves into their stage crew status.

"Um . . . ," they both said, looking at Francie. "Not sure."

"Mm mmf," Francie mumbled, mouth full.

"What, all three of you? Not sure? Why? Are you all hot on the trail of another mystery already? I mean, I heard you caught another murderer, Francie—already. Almost kind of weird how many murderers you seem to run into."

How did she hear about that already? Francie wondered but didn't ask.

"It was on the news," Phoebe chirped, answering Francie's unasked question.

Francie groaned. She could imagine the headline: "Northwoods Nancy Drew Nabs Murderous Smuggler in Underground Tunnel," or something like that. Even though it all happened only a few days before, it already seemed like months—or even years—ago. The only good thing that had come out of that whole frightening escapade, besides catching a murderer, was that she had also finally—*finally*—come into possession of the silver box.

"Don't you like being famous?" Phoebe asked.

"Not for that," Francie said, swallowing the last of the sandwich. "You know what, Pheeb?" she said, changing the subject. "You are absolutely perfect to play either the princess or the queen in *Sleeping Beauty*."

"Well, thanks. But I can only play one at a time," Phoebe said, flashing her dazzling white smile.

There was an awkward silence, and then Phoebe slid in next to Francie and said, "So. What were you all talking about before I got here? I mean, you seemed all huddled up, like maybe you were already solving another mystery."

"Uh, no. Just talking about how jolly the lunch ladies seem today."

Phoebe turned around to look at the lunch line, and as soon as she did, the three friends looked at each other with dismay. Jay mouthed, "Library."

When Phoebe turned back, each one mumbled a lame excuse: "Have to go to the bathroom." "Have to pick up a notebook I left in class." "Gotta, um, call my brother before class starts." The three friends swept up their backpacks and lunches and floated away, leaving Phoebe looking befuddled. Glancing back, Francie felt a pang of guilt for ditching her.

"I don't think Phoebe is used to being snubbed," Raven said as soon as the three of them were reunited in the library.

"What was the deal? Why are *we* suddenly so interesting? We've never been worth her time before."

"I think she just wants to be part of the crime-solving team," Raven said.

"But, why?" Jay asked. "My guess is that she just wants to blab to her real friends what we are up to. All in the service of gossip. What is Detective Francie Frye up to now?"

"The truth is, no matter what her motives are," Francie said, "and let's just be kind and assume that they're honorable, we can't let any more people in on this." Francie thought but didn't say, *It's my mystery about my life, and it's one thing to include two people who saved my life and are my best friends, and quite another to include someone who might only be interested in having gossip to share.*

"So, what do you think?" Jay said. "The museum? We can go there today after school."

Francie paused, once again contemplating her brother's warning. Then she thought of him in New York City, probably eating at fancy restaurants while she was staring down a sloppy joe in the school cafeteria. Plus they were not going to get anywhere if they couldn't get the box open. Besides, what possible harm could it do? She was hard-pressed to imagine a county historical museum as a hotbed of skulduggery.

"Skulduggery," she mumbled, pleased with the word.

"What?" Jay said.

"Nothing," Francie said. And anyway, she had to do something, or she would get pants-on-fire antsy. "What the heck," she said. "Sure."

8

AT THE MUSEUM

It was four o'clock by the time the friends walked through town on their way to the museum. Already dark outside. And snowing tiny, glittery flakes. Streets quiet—empty now, unlike the summer tourist season when crowds shuffled up and down the main street eating ice cream cones and staring into store windows at bear-bedecked lamps and moose-adorned throw pillows.

Francie imagined Theo in midtown Manhattan, where the big department stores would have their windows filled with robotic Santas and flying reindeer and everything twinkly with lights. The sidewalks would be bustling with people in chic clothes, and the streets crammed with honking cars, taxis, bikes, and buses.

"Does it always snow like this in November?" Francie asked.

"No, you're just lucky, I guess," Raven said.

Was she lucky? Maybe she was, Francie thought, as she looked around at the snow, twinkling more than any Manhattan store window. Well, maybe not *more* than, but more *magical* than. Because this was nature's sparkle. It was real, and right now, it was everywhere: the whole town was draped with a shimmering blanket of snow, including the tiny twinkling evergreen trees that seemed to sprout from every outdoor pot and window box.

A bell on the door to the museum jangled as the three of them stepped inside.

An S-shaped woman slithered over to them. "Yessss?" she said as acidly as if they'd just walked into her house unannounced. "Can I help you?" she said, squinting over her reading glasses, her eyes settling on Raven.

Francie should have been used to this by now—Raven got this look a lot—a look like, *Who let you off the reservation?* But she was always shocked every time it happened and impressed at how calmly Raven handled it.

"We're not here to steal anything," Raven said, smiling reassuringly.

"Uh, you're open, right?" Jay said. "The hours on the door said open until five."

"Those are our summer hours. Now we're on winter hours."

"Oh," Jay said. "What are those?"

"There aren't any," the woman said tersely. "We're closed." She started to swing the door shut, but Jay said quickly, "Is Mr. T. here?"

"Toad!" the woman shouted over her shoulder.

A round, red-cheeked man wearing a Hawaiian shirt under a down vest appeared behind the woman blocking the door.

"Come in! Come in!" he said, waving the kids inside. "I'm happy to show you around."

The woman moved aside only enough to let the kids sneak by

her into the museum. "I'll be locking up soon, so you don't have a lot of time," she warned them, as they sidled past.

"What kind of things are you kids interested in?" the man said, flipping his salt-and-pepper ponytail over his shoulder. "Are you studying something at school that you need to look at?" Without waiting for answers, he gestured to them to follow him. "First you've got to see this. Someone donated this stone knife from Bhutan. It doesn't really fit in our collection, but isn't it a beauty?" He pointed to an alarmingly lethal-looking knife sitting on top of a glass display case. "Go ahead! You can touch it. It won't break. It's stone. Lift it!" he commanded. "Feel how heavy it is?"

They nodded and each dutifully hefted the slightly scary artifact. As the last to hold the knife, Francie wondered what to do with it, while the man went on telling them about the other things in the case. While he chattered on, Francie glanced over at the museum lady who was sliding into her coat.

Francie set the knife carefully on top of the glass counter and wondered how she might introduce the topic of the silver box, preferably without the museum lady knowing about it.

"I'm Todd Torgelson, by the way," the man said, "but you can call me Toad. Or Mr. T., if Toad is too weird for you." Without pausing for breath, he went on, describing the contents of the museum. "In these cases there are items that are early settler–type stuff and some logging artifacts. And then the natural history section back here . . ." He led them toward the back of the museum where an entire wall was devoted to a big glass case full of taxidermied animals and birds. "And of course we have a lot of photographs, all taken in this area in the past."

The three friends peered at photos of dour-faced women in long coats and completely impractical hats teetering on the tops of their heads. A hunter with his foot on a moose carcass holding up its rack for the camera. A group of fishermen looking smug and proud on the back of a caboose with long stringers of fish draped like bunting along the railing. A sledge pulled by two white draft horses, piled high with logs so huge that the lumberjacks standing on top of the load looked like tiny toys.

And then the next photograph: a dozen dead timber wolves hanging from a pole strung between trees. The room seemed to spin under Francie's feet. The picture made her feel a little nauseous.

"It's a wonder there's anything still alive in the forest," Raven said, peering over her shoulder.

"Why did they all have to kill so *many* of everything—so many wolves. And there must be a hundred fish in that picture." Francie pointed at the photo of stringers and stringers of fish. "And a few dozen ducks in that one."

"I think there was so much abundance, it just seemed the supply was endless," Mr. T. said.

"Well, good thing we don't do that anymore," Jay said.

Francie and her friends peered into a case full of butterflies whose bodies and wings had been impaled by pins, as if the collector had been afraid they might somehow escape.

"Right," Raven said. "Now we kill them off by destroying habitat and with pesticides and climate change."

A throat being cleared caused them all to swivel toward the front desk where the older woman was straightening papers. "I'll be locking up in ten minutes," she said curtly.

"Let me show you . . ." Mr. T. waved at the three friends to follow him.

"To be honest," Francie said, "we didn't actually come to see the museum." Finding that she didn't want to hurt Mr. T.'s feelings, she added, "As interesting as it is."

"We're hoping you can help us with a puzzle box," Jay said.

"Reeaally?" Mr. T. said, almost squeaking with excitement. "Do you have it with you?" His fingers literally twitched as he held his hands out, hoping to receive the box.

Raven and Jay nodded, but Francie hesitated, not wanting the lady to see it.

"Let's go in the office," Mr. T. said, starting for a door toward the back of the room.

The office, a large room in the back of the building, was filled with old wooden file cabinets, cardboard boxes, a couple of library-sized desks, various display cases, and a rather large taxidermied black bear standing on its haunches, teeth bared. A couple of electric space heaters pumped warm air into the place.

Francie set the box down on one of the desks, then unzipped her parka and pulled off her stocking hat.

"Wow," Mr. T. stared at her hair. "You're . . . are you . . . I used to know . . ."

Francie's heart beat haphazardly. "My mother? Iris Frye?" she managed to ask.

"You're the spitting image," he said. "I was sorry to hear . . ." He trailed off as he started digging through files in one of the old cabinets.

Francie wondered what she could ask him that would reveal something about her mother, but before she could think of anything, he emerged, holding a photo of a box. "Of course, you should have it checked out by a real expert," he said, "but comparing it to this print, I would say the box is an antique silver Japanese puzzle box. Not terribly old, nineteenth-century, worth a couple hundred dollars maybe."

"That's all?" Francie said. *Well, if that's all it's worth, it isn't the box itself that's so valuable,* she thought. *It has to be what's in it.*

Mr. T. rubbed his hands together, wiggled his eyebrows, and

said, "Let's see if we can get this puppy open!" He picked up a magnifying glass and began to examine the box with it, something Francie had not thought to do.

"I knew your mother when we were both kids," he said to Francie as he squinted at the box. "My parents had a place on Enchantment. She stayed with her aunts out there in that cabin I think they still have."

Francie nodded and said, "Yes, they still own that cabin."

"We used to play together," he said. He paused to examine the underside of the box. "But nothing was just an ordinary game to her. Not even hide-and-seek. Even that wasn't ordinary. She left clues."

"Clues?" Francie asked. "What kind of clues?"

"Written clues, sometimes," he said. "A little note scratched on a scrap of birch bark. Or little arrows made out of sticks, a ribbon on a branch." As he talked his hands played over the box. "She had to," he went on, "because she kept moving. She'd be a step ahead of you, watching you look for her. Or maybe she had it all figured out in advance, I don't know."

Francie tried to keep her focus on his hands, but her mind whizzed. Clues, she thought. Had her mother left clues for her? If she had, would Francie notice them? Would she know how to interpret them?

"Your mom was the one who got me interested in puzzles," Mr. T. went on. "Everything was a puzzle to her. Or a game of hide-and-seek." He grew quiet. His face wore a look of deep concentration. "See this?" he said. They leaned closer. He pointed to a tiny image on the box. "See this island?" he said. "Or I guess it could be a peninsula—hard to tell."

"Island?" Francie said, leaning closer.

"Yes," he said. "On this lake."

"A lake?" Francie repeated. "An island?" Her heart rang like a gong someone had struck with a big hammer. How had she missed seeing a lake and an island?

He handed her the magnifying glass, which she had to adjust until she saw what he was describing. In the midst of the forest, nearly hidden by trees, a lake, and what could be interpreted as an island in the midst of it.

"And there's a church. You can tell because—see?—that's a steeple."

Francie couldn't help but steal a glance at Raven. Seeing her glance, Raven mouthed the word "Crazy!"

"So," Mr. T. said, rubbing his hands together, "this is a story puzzle box. There's a story that goes with it, and you need to know the story in order to make the moves in the right order."

The gong that was Francie's heart continued to reverberate.

"Does anybody know the story?" Mr. T. was saying just as the museum lady barged into the office.

"Locking up!" she barked.

The foursome spun around to see the crabby lady standing at the door, hands on hips. Francie stepped in front of the box to shield it from the woman's view.

"Can we come back tomorrow?" Jay asked.

"I won't be here," Mr. T. explained. "I'm going to a conference. But I could take the box with me . . ." He reached toward it, but Francie snatched it up.

"I'm sorry," Francie said. "That isn't possible." She hurriedly shoved the box into her backpack.

"Everybody out!" the museum lady screeched.

"Aw, come on," Mr. T. begged. "Just a few more minutes. I can lock up myself."

"No," she said. "Locking up is my job. I can't trust you to do it properly."

"I'm not a five-year-old!" Mr. T.'s face grew red.

"Then you shouldn't act like one," the lady snapped.

"We better go," Francie said, moving out of the office, her friends following. As they hustled through the museum and out the front door, the sounds of an escalating argument trailed behind them.

The threesome stepped out into the late November afternoon, or more like evening—not even 5 p.m. and night had descended. The scent of damp leaves, wet pavement, and melting snow swept away the musty smell of the museum. Even the night seemed to have its own smell, Francie thought. Maybe it was the smell of darkness.

Francie zipped up her jacket and linked arms with her friends, one on each side of her, and felt their steady presence as they walked the quiet streets toward home.

"Should we try to get the box open ourselves?" Raven said. "At least knowing something now?"

"What do we know?" Jay asked, looking from one to the other.

Raven started to explain, but Francie stopped her. "Let's talk about it tomorrow," she said. She needed a night alone with the box and her thoughts.

"Um . . . ," Raven said. "Don't look now, but do you feel like we're being followed?" She tilted her head to indicate something behind them. "Big black car."

Jay glanced over his shoulder. "Probably just out-of-towners trying to find a restaurant that's actually open." He laughed. "This town is so small the main street dead-ends in both directions."

"It's so small the city limit signs are both on the same post," Raven continued.

"They call the jail *amoeba* 'cause it only has one cell," Jay joked.

Francie laughed half-heartedly, and then her friends, without discussing it, their arms still linked with hers, cut through an alley, ducked between buildings, and jogged through a few backyards, finally stopping at Francie's apartment.

"Are you sure you're going to be okay all by yourself?" Raven said, looking up at the big house divided into four apartments. "You can come stay at my house, you know. Or if you want, I can stay with you."

"I'll be fine," Francie said. "I'll see you guys tomorrow at school."

GRANDDAD INTERFERES

"Far, far away there is a lake," Francie mumbled as she unlocked her apartment, stumbled inside, locked the door behind her, and tossed the keys on the small table inside the door. She flipped on the lamp, pulled the box out of her backpack, and carried it to the kitchen table. While she slid out of her jacket she wondered how she had missed noticing the island and the church on the island. Examining it more closely, she saw you had to really look to see all of that. The same trees that obscured the lake and the island also obscured the tiny church and its tiny steeple. Once you knew it was there, though, you could see it.

When she heard Theo's phone ring, her first thought was, *Why is Theo's phone in my pocket?* Then she remembered that Theo's phone was now hers, and she dug it out of her jacket pocket and answered it.

"I've tried calling you a bunch of times," Theo said. "How come you don't answer?"

"Sorry, busy," Francie said. "Going to shows, fancy restaurants, you know how it is here in Walpurgis."

"So, how's it really going?" he asked.

"More split ends than usual," she said.

"Do you have the box well hidden? You haven't been showing it to your friends at school, right?"

"Of course not!" Francie said, turning the box round and round on the table.

"Or anyone else?" Theo said. "I'm serious. There are people looking for that box. They could be—probably are—dangerous."

"Right," Francie said, wondering what she should tell him. Should she let him know that the box itself was not valuable? If she did, she'd have to admit she'd shown it to someone, and Theo would probably be mad at her, so she kept that to herself. There'd be time for explaining later.

"Surgery went fine. Granddad's doing well. Crotchety as ever," Theo said.

"Uh huh," Francie mumbled. *Far, far away there is a lake*, she thought, letting her fingers move along the part of the box that represented a lake, then pressing, and feeling a slight give, as if the "water" in the lake had moved. She gasped.

"What?" Theo said.

"Nothing," Francie said. "Go on."

Theo went on about the ins and outs of Granddad's shoulder surgery.

On the lake there is an island.

"What did you do at the cabin?" Theo asked. "Why did you stay there? You should have come with us, Frenchy."

Francie's fingers played along the island, pressing, twisting, poking . . .

When she didn't answer, he said, "It was a lot to ask Sandy to come back for you."

Maybe, she thought, but she knew Sandy would do anything for her. He'd always been like that since they were little. And he still blushed furiously every time he saw her. "He didn't mind," she said.

"No doubt," Theo said dryly. "How does Nels feel about that?"

"Sandy is not my boyfriend." Francie suddenly felt the island shift, like a tiny earthquake. Instead of a rift in the earth, though, a panel slid open, revealing a tiny key. "Holy Zamboni," she whispered.

Suddenly her grandfather's voice came over the phone. "Francesca?"

"Yes, it's me."

"You're grounded."

"What? Why?" She let the box sit for a moment while she concentrated on the phone call.

"Let's call it a preemptive strike," Granddad said. "Anyway, I assume you've done plenty of things you should have been grounded for already, and if you haven't, you will."

Francie couldn't really argue with that, so she didn't.

Next it was Theo's voice again. "Hi, it's me."

"What was that about?" Francie asked.

"I think he's just worried about you and trying to keep you out of danger."

The big, black car from earlier in the evening drove slowly through Francie's mind. But what could Granddad or Theo do about it? So she didn't say anything.

"Francesca!" Granddad was back on the phone. "Did you hear what I said? Now remember, when you're out and about, keep your eyes open and your head swiveling around. Try to remember the faces and cars you see. If someone is following you, the sooner you realize it, the more options you have to evade them.

If you feel endangered, make your way to a public place and call law enforcement. Goodbye."

The line went dead. Francie stared at the phone for a moment, shook her head, and focused her attention back on the box.

"On the island is a church," Francie said as she ran her fingers along the steeple peeking out from the trees. She tried pushing, poking, and then sliding, and she found that, with a bit of pressure from her fingers, the steeple slid up, just enough to reveal a keyhole. Francie picked up the tiny key, inserted it into the keyhole, and turned.

The lid clicked open.

10

GREEN JELLY BEANS

"AND . . . ?" Raven said, leaning forward, her delicious-looking veggie sandwich inches from Francie's mouth. "What was in it? Tell us!"

"Yes, come on, tell us!" Jay said from their lepers-only spot at the far end of the cafeteria.

"Nothing!" Francie said, leaning back and crossing her arms across her chest. "Nothing."

"Nothing?" Jay and Raven cackled in unison.

"The box was empty."

Her friends' shoulders drooped. Jay frowned. Raven tossed her sandwich down.

"Aren't you going to eat that?" Francie said, reaching for it.

"Yes!" Raven yelped, snatching it up again. Then she relented and gave Francie half. "There," she said, "consolation prize."

Before Raven could change her mind, Francie took an enormous bite, savoring the chewiness of the homemade wheat bread, the creamy avocado and juicy tomato, and the crunch of the lettuce. It tasted just the way you would think a sandwich made by a mom would taste—full of love.

What Francie didn't tell her friends, maybe because she wasn't sure how she could describe it, or maybe because they would think she was cuckoo: the box wasn't totally empty. As soon as she opened it, a smell, a scent both exotic yet familiar rushed out.

"But, geez!" Jay said. "You figured out how to open it. That is pretty amazing."

Francie nodded, thinking how surprisingly simple it had been once she figured it out. But had it been simple because she really had known how all along? Each time she had pressed a button or slid a panel or twisted a gizmo, she had thought, *Oh yes, that's right,* as if she'd done it before. Almost like déjà vu.

Like the scent of the box, which she felt she had smelled before. She had held it to her face and inhaled, over and over, trying and trying to open the lock that held her memory captive. But her mind was like a puzzle box, one that she could not figure out. Which button? What lever? Where could she press that would activate a spring and release her memories? Springing the box had not brought her any answers. Maybe the only way to find her mother was to open her memory and plumb the depths. But how?

"Well, that's a bummer," Jay said. "But, oh hey! I almost forgot. I found your mysterious Loretta Swift."

Francie stopped midchew to stare at Jay, then gulped her mouthful down, and asked, "Where?"

"The place is called Birch Grove," Jay answered.

All fall an old woman who maybe held the answer to Francie's lifelong question had been living just blocks away from her. *All fall*, Francie thought, as she and Raven walked to the nearby nursing home. Francie had been barely able to concentrate the rest of the school day until she and Raven could go to the nursing home and meet her.

"Loretta, you have some visitors!" the nurse's aide chirped, then backed out of the room to let the girls enter.

This could be it, Francie thought, fizzy with excitement. She was about to meet the woman who knew things. Maybe everything. The woman who might open the puzzle box that was Francie's life.

Francie found herself holding her breath as she stepped into the small, sunlit room.

Backlit by the afternoon sun, the old woman's white hair seemed to glow. Her face was familiar to Francie, but only in a vague way. And yet there was an almost electrical charge up Francie's arm as she shook Loretta's small hand.

Francie would have expected someone who had spent her life out in the woods, carrying her water and chopping her own wood, to be hale and hearty, and maybe as big as a man. But Loretta was almost sparrow-like. Not tiny or fragile. The impression came from the way she fluttered her hands, tilted her head, her quickness. It almost seemed to Francie that if the old woman had enough space, she could lift up out of her wheelchair into the air and perch on the ceiling fixture.

Loretta smiled big and sang out, "Iris!"

The name stopped Francie in her tracks. "Iris is—was—my mother's name," she managed to choke out.

"Oh, so you're her daughter?" Loretta asked.

"Yes," Francie said. "My name is Francesca, but everyone calls me Francie. Or, well, some of my friends call me Frenchy. This is my friend Raven."

"Raven," the old woman repeated. She let out the typical gurgling chortle of a raven, then laughed. "I suppose you get that a lot," she said to Raven.

"I don't know if I've ever heard anybody do it as well as you," Raven admitted.

"Sit down, sit down," Loretta said.

The two girls sat next to each other on the neatly made bed.

"Have some jelly beans," the old woman said, extending a bowl of dusty multicolored candy. Francie declined, but Raven dug below the top layer and took a small handful.

Loretta settled back into her wheelchair and said, "It's so nice to see you, Iris! I can't remember the last time. It had to be quite a while ago."

"I'm Francie," Francie reminded her.

"Francie," Loretta repeated. "And who is your friend?"

"This is Raven," Francie said, with a sinking feeling. Then, in order to prevent another raven call, she quickly added, "You must have known my mother, Iris."

"Oh, she was your mother?"

Francie nodded.

"And what is your name?"

Francie and Raven looked at one another. "I'm getting dizzy," Raven mumbled around the jelly beans.

Francie's earlier fizz of anticipation turned flat, with an added bitter bite of disappointment.

"Have some jelly beans," Loretta said, extending the bowl of candy again. "I like the yellow ones. I think the nurses do, too," she whispered. "That's why there are so few of them in there." She cast a dark look at the door, then turned, smiling, to Francie. "You liked the green ones," she said, pointing to a green one in the bowl.

Francie did not remember that she liked green jelly beans, but she figured she better take one, so she did, adding, "Thank you."

Loretta set the bowl on the table and settled back in her chair again. Francie held the jelly bean between her fingers, not sure whether to eat it or not.

"I love your hair, Loretta," Raven said. "It's so long!"

Loretta patted her hair at the mention of it. "I used to braid it and wear it wrapped around my head, you know, like this." She crisscrossed her fingers to show how her long braids circled her head. "But my fingers aren't so nimble anymore." She held out her hands, knotted with arthritis.

"Can I braid it for you?" Raven said, jumping up. She took the brush from the dresser and moved behind Loretta's chair.

Francie watched with wonder as Raven gently pulled the brush through the old woman's long tresses. Loretta's face softened, her eyes closed, as she relaxed under Raven's gentle touch. Francie sat with her hands in her lap, feeling cold, wondering, would a mother have taught her how to show kindness in this way?

"So nice of you to stop by, Iris," Loretta said, and Francie felt that itchy feeling behind her eyes that meant she might start to cry—all her high hopes about this meeting dashed.

Neither she nor Raven bothered to correct Loretta. Instead, Raven asked the older woman if she'd always had long hair. While the two discussed this, Francie looked down at the jelly bean in her hand, then popped it in her mouth. It tasted not like fake lime or asparagus or avocado or some other weird green thing but of summer air, sunshine, sweet herbs, and tender wildflowers. It tasted like the herb-filled cabin, of sunshine slanting in through the open door, across the wide plank floor, over the rag rug, and warming the back of a little girl's legs as she stood playing with a small, silver box. It tasted, Francie thought, the way the silver box smelled.

The memory faded with the last of the taste of the jelly bean, and while Raven pinned the braids in a circle around the old woman's head, Francie picked out another green one and popped it in her mouth.

Once again, the taste brought her back to the cabin, back to the sunshine on her legs. *She'd been crying. Crying because her mother was going to leave her there. The old woman had given Francie the box, her hands calloused, yet somehow soft. "See if you can open this," the old woman said. "Such a clever girl!"*

If she could solve the mystery of the box, maybe her mother would appear and take her home. That was what she had thought then. Maybe her mother would come back . . .

Maybe the box had not been her mother's, Francie thought now. Maybe it was the old woman's, but in her mind Francie had indelibly linked it to her mother, believing it could bring her mother back to her. She still believed that if she could solve the mystery of the box, her mother would come back to her.

"Is there something magic about these jelly beans?" Francie asked.

"Oh, they're just ordinary candy," Loretta said. "The magic is that the taste of something brings back memories, don't you think? Each color a little shot. That's why I like them—because my memory is not very good anymore," she stated. "I don't know if you noticed."

While Loretta talked, Francie popped another green jelly bean into her mouth, but now it just tasted like mint, and no more memories came. "How do I get my memory to work better?" she mumbled.

"You're asking *me*?" Loretta howled and slapped her thigh.

"I think she's asking the universe," Raven said.

"Loretta, I need to ask you something. When Iris brought the little girl—the little girl who was me—to your house, where did she go? Where was Iris going?"

Loretta looked confused for a moment, then she looked thoughtful. She repeated to herself, "Where was Iris going? Where was Iris going?" under her breath, maybe so she wouldn't forget what she was trying to remember. While she muttered she dug around in the candy bowl until she triumphantly held up a yellow jelly bean.

"Ha!" she said, leaning forward conspiratorially. "Those people," she nodded toward the hallway, "they come in here when I'm not looking and take the yellow ones."

"Do you remember?" Francie said.

"Remember what?"

"Where Iris was going when she left the little girl—me—at your house?"

"You're Iris's little girl?" Loretta said, adding, "All grown up now."

Francie resisted frustration and asked, "Why did my mother leave me at your house?"

"Thieves," Loretta said in a low whisper that made Francie and Raven lean forward.

"Thieves?" Francie repeated. She pictured Loretta's ramshackle cottage, its simplicity, its obvious poverty. "What were the thieves after?"

"Plants," Loretta whispered.

The door opened and an aide came in carrying a small plastic cup filled with what looked like jelly beans but Francie realized were pills.

"Time for meds," the aide said, handing Loretta the little cup and a glass of water.

Loretta threw back the pills, swallowed, and made a gagging face at the girls. Then she said, "I want to read you something." She opened to a bookmarked page and said, "This is by a poet named Mary Oliver. If you want truth telling, read poetry!" Clutching the bookmark in her hand, she didn't read from the book, but said, "Mary Oliver once said, 'If I have any lasting worth it will be because I have tried to make people remember what the Earth is meant to look like.'"

She shut the book and looked out the window for a moment. A birdfeeder was busy with chickadees and nuthatches—birds Francie had learned about from her aunts, the hardy ones that stuck it out all winter here in the north.

"That's about the only thing I can remember," Loretta said, then tipped her face to look at them. "'What the Earth is meant to look like.' But since I am old and not long for the world, you young people have to do it. You have to remember what the Earth is now. Remember what it looks like now, and try to imagine what it's meant to be."

Francie and Raven were quiet, thinking that through.

Loretta went on. "And you young people will have to somehow strive to save what you can." She looked up at Raven whose hand was resting on Loretta's shoulder. "Such a pretty girl," she said, patting Raven's hand.

"And I want *you* to have this," she almost whispered to Francie, pressing the bookmark into Francie's hands.

"Okay, Loretta," the aide chirped, grasping the handles of her wheelchair and starting for the door. "Time for dinner!"

Outside the nursing home, Raven and Francie tucked their hands under their armpits and their heads down into their jackets and walked against the wind to Vi's Café where they had arranged to meet Jay.

Jay sat in a booth in the corner, hunched over his laptop.

Raven and Francie slid in across from him.

Vi came by and handed them menus. The older woman stopped, slipped off her glasses, letting them dangle from the glittery chain around her neck, and gave the threesome a good looking-at. "You kiddos look like you could use some hot choco-late," she said. "Am I right?"

Francie agreed, adding, "I'm buying. Theo gave me some cash," she explained.

While they waited, they told Jay what had transpired at the nursing home.

"What do you think she was talking about? Plant thieves?" Raven said.

"Maybe she's just a loopy old lady," Jay suggested.

"Or paranoid," Francie said. "She thought the nurses were stealing her yellow jelly beans, but obviously she just forgot that she'd been eating them herself."

Raven shook her head. "No, you're wrong. She has some memory problems, but she isn't crazy. For instance, she told me I was pretty." She batted her eyelashes and opened her menu.

Francie remembered that when she'd first met Raven, she'd thought she was kind of ordinary looking, and that her name should have been Sparrow, because she seemed like the kind of person who didn't want to be noticed. Now that she knew Raven, though, Francie agreed that she was startlingly pretty. Raven's glossy hair hung in a thick dark braid down her back, set off by a pair of the colorful beaded earrings Raven's grandmother made. When Raven looked up from the menu, Francie was reminded of her most stunning feature, her eyes, which Francie had learned were all-seeing. Raven noticed things, and she remembered what she'd seen.

"Loretta got that right," Francie said. "But I still don't get what she was talking about when she said that my mom left me at her cabin because of plant thieves. Like, what kind of plants?"

"What do you think those guys were doing out at her place when we were there?" Raven said. "Helping themselves to spruce tops and balsam boughs from either her private property or a state forest without a permit, I'd guess. Given that they were hiding stuff in Loretta's house, I kinda doubt they were doing it legally."

"As illegal as that might be, it hardly seems like something that would send my mother into hiding for most of my life!" Francie said.

"Maybe some other kind of plant?" Jay ventured. "Like lady's slippers? People dig them up out of state parks and even private property."

Vi, returning with three mugs of hot chocolate, just the way they liked it, crammed with marshmallows, added, "Which is really stupid, because they just die if you try to transplant them. I learned that the hard way." Vi went on, as if she'd been part of the conversation, "Also, disturbing the plant often kills the whole thing, even the part left behind."

Francie wondered how much of what they'd said Vi had heard, but there was nothing to be done about it now. And Vi was a good soul, treating all the kids who came in as if they were her own, asking if they'd done their homework, how school was going, whether they were going to the dance on Saturday.

"Maybe there's something we're not thinking of," Jay said.

"Oh!" Francie said. "Loretta gave me this." Francie took the bookmark from her pocket and set it on the table. It was a simple strip of gray, heavyweight paper decorated by the painted image of a single flower, a delicate plant consisting of stem, leaves, and dainty blue petals around a pale purplish center.

"Hey, though!" Raven blurted out.

The others looked at her.

"I just had a thought," Raven explained. "I mean, maybe this is the plant Loretta was talking about. The one the thieves were after!"

"What kind of plant is it?" Francie asked, looking at the others.

Raven shook her head.

Vi shrugged.

Jay was staring at his laptop, already Googling it.

"If you've got questions about stuff like this, you should probably talk to Buzz over there at the DNR," Vi said.

"What's the DNR?" Francie asked.

"Oh, honey," Vi said, patting her arm sympathetically. "You're really not from around here, are you?"

Buzz, a Department of Natural Resources conservation officer, was out in the field, so he answered their call while driving the back roads in his truck.

Jay put the phone on speaker. "We've got a couple of questions," he said. "For one thing, we're wondering about theft of plants from public lands."

Raven and Francie leaned closer to the phone to listen.

"Here's the thing," Buzz shouted over the sound of his truck. "Public lands are public. You have the right to go out and pick some mushrooms for your dinner. You are welcome to pick blueberries and bake some pies for your family. You can get a permit to cut boughs or a Christmas tree for your own personal enjoyment—or to sell, if you have permit. But going into public lands and cutting trees without a permit, taking birch bark, berries, or what have you to sell commercially—that is illegal, and what it is, is stealing from everyone. Stealing your right to go in and enjoy this public resource as a healthy, ecologically sound environment."

"So do people steal things from state forests and stuff?" Jay asked.

"Oh, yeah," Buzz shouted over the noise of the engine. "That's a real problem. Not just here, but all over the place. People steal or gather all kinds of things from public lands without permits. Thousands and thousands of succulents have been stolen along the California coast. It takes a long time for succulents to get big, so large ones are in demand. In the southwest it's saguaro cacti. Same kind of thing. It takes so long for saguaro to get big—ten years just to grow one inch! One hundred years before they even start to grow one of those goofy arms. Saguaro cacti are the most stolen plant in the country. As for around here, there are all kinds of things: mushrooms, berries, wildflowers, lady's slippers, prince's pine, birch bark, birch trees . . ."

"Birch trees?" Jay asked.

"Yep," Buzz said. "People cut young birch saplings. Whole stands of birch. And once those saplings are gone, the aspen spring up, and that's the end of the birch forest—destroyed forever. For the sake of home decor."

"Home décor?" Raven said.

"Silly, really, because if you've ever put a birch sapling in a room, you'll notice it doesn't smell very good. Stinky, really."

"What about taking plants from private property?"

"Of course that is stealing, too! Plenty of people have had their private property trees cut down by logging companies that claim to have 'mistaken' the property line . . . ."

The conservation officer went on, but Francie was thinking about something else. Although it was sad that people stole plants to the point of destroying ecosystems, she just couldn't see how any of these offenses would cause her mother to fake her death and go underground for more than a dozen years.

"Ask about the flower," she told Jay.

"We're going to send you a picture of a flower," he said. "When you have time, can you look at it and let us know what it is?"

"Sure," he said, "I'll look at it, but I gotta warn you, I'm going to be out of cell range any—"

The phone went dead. The three friends looked at each other and shrugged.

"I'm sure he'll be in touch as soon as he can take a look," Jay said.

"Yeah," Francie agreed, and all three slurped up the chocolaty goodness at the bottom of their mugs of cocoa.

II

HIDING THE BOX

FRANCIE SET THE BOOKMARK on the kitchen table and looked at it from various angles, as if that might help her to identify the pictured flower. She would ask her biology teacher, Mr. Blondeau, the next day, she thought, until she remembered her class would not be in school: they were leaving on a field trip, at like six o'clock in the morning.

She picked up the form explaining the trip. "Six a.m.," she groaned but then perked up considerably when she saw where they were going. First stop, Minneapolis Institute of Art, then after lunch, Como Park Conservatory. A conservatory! A place full of plants! Plants of all kinds! And people who knew about them!

Francie did a little jig and then, out of sheer excitement, filled out the permission slip for the parents and signed, not one of her aunts' or her grandfather's names, as she usually did. This time on a whim she signed her mother's name—just to see what it felt like.

Iris Frye, she wrote, in a nice, flowy script, quite unlike her own chicken-scratch handwriting.

Then she opened the fridge and stared into its vast emptiness. Things were bad in the food department. And things were pretty bad when she was resting all her hopes of finding her mother on a chance bookmark from a loopy old lady, she thought, as she examined the pathetic excuse for food in the refrigerator. A quart of probably sour milk, a jar of olives, an ancient box of takeout something-she-didn't-want-to-know-about.

The phone rang. She closed the fridge and picked up the phone. Granddad. Steeling herself, she answered.

"Where is that box Theo tells me about?" her grandfather asked.

"Hidden," she answered, assuming that was the next thing he would demand. She picked up the box, which was still sitting on the kitchen table where she had left it—and looked around the room, wondering where to put it.

Theo's voice was next. "Granddad couldn't hear what you said. What did you say?"

"I said it is hidden!" She stuck the box in the microwave and firmly shut the door.

"Okay, good," Theo said, then went back into his litany of not showing the box to anyone: *Blah blah blah . . . .*

She opened the refrigerator again hoping that some delicious thing had magically appeared there.

"Tell her not to go to school tomorrow," her grandfather was saying in the background. Then his voice came over the line. "Francesca? Did you hear me?"

"Yes, but I'm signed up for a field trip."

"I don't know what a feed drip is, but just stay home."

The line went dead.

She probably should have explained to Granddad and Theo

that they were all wound up about nothing. The box was a big, fat nothing. And anyway, she'd be on a bus with dozens of other seniors, their art teacher, and a bunch of chaperones. Once they got to the Cities, she'd be with the whole group, most of the time inside an art museum or a plant conservatory. What could possibly go wrong?

12
THE INSTITUTE OF ART

AMID A DARK WOODS with pale poppies growing at her feet, a girl barely lifts the lid of a golden box. She seems apprehensive yet so curious that she can't resist—and is maybe a little hopeful about—what she'll find.

"The title of the painting is *Psyche Opening the Golden Box*, concerning the Greek myth," the guide told Francie's group, all huddled together like a herd of sheep. "By John William Waterhouse."

Psyche, Psyche . . . , Francie thought. *Wasn't she the one who was in love with Cupid?*

"In order to prove she was worthy of Cupid," the guide went on, gesturing toward the painting, "Psyche was challenged by Cupid's mother, Venus, to do several impossible tasks. The last task was to retrieve a box from the underworld and bring it to Venus. The box was supposed to contain a dose of the beauty of Persephone, queen of the underworld. Psyche was forbidden to open it, but she couldn't resist. She opened it and thereupon fell into a Stygian sleep."

"A what-gian sleep?" one of Francie's classmates asked.

"*Stygian. Dark and gloomy, hellish,*" Jay said, reading the definition off his phone.

"That's right," the guide said.

"It's the Sleeping Beauty story, right?" Ms. Hanover said. "Psyche falls into a long sleep, but Cupid wakes her with a kiss, isn't that it? Don't forget everybody"—Ms. Hanover called out—"all of you sleepy beauties and handsome princes can still try out for the play!"

There were a few muffled groans. The guide cleared his throat, then continued, "The story goes that Cupid drew the sleep from Psyche's face and placed it in the box. Then he pricked her with an arrow that did no harm, lifted her in the air, and took her to present the box to Venus. The story ends happily with the wedding of Cupid and Psyche."

"Or you can be part of the stage crew," Ms. Hanover continued, apparently not quite finished with her announcement. "The costumes and set are going to be wonderful!"

"Moving on . . . ," the guide said and motioned for the group to follow him.

Her classmates moved on, but Francie stepped closer and gazed at the painting. The sounds of their chatter faded and soon there were just voices echoing from distant galleries. She felt a kind of kinship with the girl in the painting; she understood the longing on her face. The hopefulness. And her fascination with that box. Being here without the box in her backpack or nearby made Francie feel a little bit . . . she wasn't sure . . . almost panicky. Studying the painting, at Psyche barely peeking into her box, Francie felt a longing to be holding her own box in just such a way.

"Francie!" The sharp clicking of heels on the parquet floor and a harsh whisper got her attention. Francie tore her gaze away from the painting and turned to see the art teacher gesturing to her from the door of the gallery. "We're waiting for you," Ms. Hanover said.

For the rest of the tour Francie gazed unseeing at the sculptures, paintings, furnishings. All she could think of was the girl in the clinging pink gown, peeking into the box just long enough to let the sleep out.

"Raven," she whispered as Raven pulled her along through the galleries, past somber dark oil paintings and cool white marble statues. "You know that painting of Psyche? Something like that must have happened to me."

"Something like what?"

"Maybe that box sent me into a Stygian sleep, like Psyche," Francie said, "because for some reason I couldn't remember anything about it for so long. And maybe my mother suffered the same fate. What if she lost her memory and has been wandering around for the past thirteen years?"

"Sounds more like something that would happen in a movie than in real life," Raven said. "Come on—we've gotten hardly anywhere with this treasure hunt assignment." She waved the worksheet at Francie.

"I just know the whole thing has something to do with memory," Francie said, as she and Raven wove in and out of various period rooms—completely furnished rooms from places like China, Japan, and England, all from different times in history. Francie began to get the dizzying feeling of being in some kind of strange time machine that plopped her into sixteenth-century England, then into a 1772 Charleston drawing room ("Who knew 'drawing room' actually meant 'withdrawing room'?" Raven said), and finally into a living room in Duluth, Minnesota, in 1906. If only she could move as fluidly among her memories as she did among these rooms!

Exiting the period rooms, the two girls came to a space in

which hung a sheer curtain printed with the image of a lake of deep blue water, surrounded by a fringe of green forest, and above the forest a paler blue sky. The curtain was hung in a half-circle, so it was possible to step inside and view the lake from the inside out, or be viewed from the outside as if floating in the lake, or perhaps as part of the lake. Francie felt she recognized the scene, yet it all seemed as ungraspable as her memories.

"I really need to remember what happened!" Francie said. "Or, remember what Mr. T. at the museum said? That my mom left clues when she played hide and seek? What if she left clues, but I just haven't picked up on them?"

"Well," Raven said, "what about that thing your mom told you about the lake and stuff? How did that little ditty go?"

"Far, far away there is a lake. On the lake is an island. On the island is a church."

"Maybe the things are meant symbolically," Raven said. "Like a lot of the art we've been hearing about today."

"Okay, how?"

"Lake represents water, which is one of the elements," Raven said. "Island represents earth, another element. Church represents . . . spirituality. The spirit."

"In the church is a well," Francie said. "What about that?"

"Hmm," Raven said. "A well is deep, right? You can't see the bottom. So maybe it represents that which we cannot know— the unknowable."

"You should get an A in Symbolism," Francie said.

"That would be great if we were being graded on that instead of this." Raven waved the worksheet at Francie again. "If we don't get started on this, we're going to flunk. How about if I take care of this"—she snatched Francie's worksheet out of her hands— "and you just do whatever it is you gotta do. You are worthless for anything else today."

Francie stared at and through the curtain, thinking. The box had a lake, an island, and a church. *I got all the way to—even into—the church, in a manner of speaking. But where's the well? What had Raven said about it? The well represents the unknowable?*

That's for sure, Francie thought. *Unknowable.*

13

COMO PARK CONSERVATORY

"THE NEXT STOP is the Como Park Conservatory," Ms. Hanover said from her spot in the front of the bus. "It's a lovely place full of plants of all kinds, and a beautiful exhibit of poinsettias and winter greenery and so on. You'll have time to sketch and take photographs. Not just selfies! This is meant to be an art project!"

The bus pulled up and the students piled out into the cold winter air, then filed into the building.

"We'll all stay together, from one room to the next," Ms. Hanover said, walking backward as the class trooped along with her. "The first is the Fern Room." She pulled open the door and they all followed her inside.

It was warm. And humid. The air was heavy and aromatic, perfumed as if with flowers. Inhaling, Francie smelled all the things the sub in English had said were missing from winter: green, growing things, decaying plant matter, warm earth.

As they moved from the fern room to the circular, high, glass-ceilinged Palm Dome, filled with tall palm trees, Francie kept her eyes out for a plant that looked like the one on the bookmark. It was for sure not in the Sunken Garden, a room with a long rectangular pool surrounded on all sides with bright pinkish-red poinsettias, nor did she find anything like it in the North Garden.

The group returned to the Palm Dome, where they were told to take a little time to sketch or take photos. Francie hunted among the plants, hoping to find one that looked like the picture on her bookmark.

Small identification labels placed near plants indicated the Latin name as well as the common name of the plants. She read: *Nepenthes x 'Miranda'*—Tropical Pitcher Plant; and *Curcuma longa*—Turmeric.

Her eye drifted to the next small sign, mostly hidden beneath a fern frond, which—she froze, staring—read: *Francesca Frye*—Francie.

Had she just seen that?

Her gaze traveled to the next little sign.

Aliquis—Someone is waiting.

Then another.

Te expectant—For you.

And then a little farther, very near the exit, one more.

Foris—Outside.

Francie glanced around. Through the foliage she could see Ms. Hanover bending over one of the students who was actually sketching. The adult chaperones were almost exclusively looking at their phones, perhaps having grown tired of looking at actual palm trees, preferring to look at pictures of them on Instagram. Or maybe they were watching cat videos, who knows?

She knew she was not allowed to leave the conservatory. But . . . would anyone even notice if she was gone for just a moment? Just to find out what this was about?

Francie backed into the Fern Room, continued down the hall past the gift shop, and then ducked outside. A big, black limo was parked on the circular drive, and leaning against it was a tall woman wearing what looked like a chauffeur's uniform, cap and all. She was holding a small white sign with a name on it. The name was . . . Francesca Frye.

Had Francie really seen that? She stepped closer.

"Francesca?" The chauffeur lady asked.

Francie nodded and the chauffeur opened the rear door and gestured to Francie to get in. "There's someone who would like to speak to you," the woman said. "I will take you there."

"I can't—" Francie gestured behind her.

"It shouldn't take long. I was told to tell you that it concerns your mother," the chauffeur said.

"My mother? How?" Francie looked at the dark interior of the car.

"I'm sorry I can't tell you more," the woman said, gesturing again for her to get into the car.

"But . . . ," Francie said, hesitating.

"Your friend can come along if you'd be more comfortable."

"Friend?" Francie glanced over her shoulder to see Raven, standing just outside the door with her arms tucked under her armpits. Francie gestured to her.

Raven jogged up to her and whispered, "Are you crazy? You can't get into some weird car!"

"I have to!" Francie said, climbing inside.

"Oh, brother," Raven said, climbing in after her. "Why, oh why can't I let you do this alone?"

A short time later, Francie found herself in another conservatory. Like the Como Park Conservatory, the entire building, several rooms long, was made of glass. But it seemed somehow even larger—maybe because it wasn't full of other visitors. In fact, the only other person there, besides Raven, was a man with a shiny, round head and a shiny, round face, as hairless as a baby bird. She immediately began thinking of him as Mr. Baldo. His hands, busy clipping stems off a shrub, were also round, the fingers as cylindrical as sausages. Dexterous sausages, she noted. The red silk kimono-style robe he wore, embroidered all over with dragons, seemed an odd gardening costume, Francie thought. But whatever. Not any odder than everything else about this scenario. Beyond the man loomed a jungle of huge-leafed plants, ferns nearly as tall as she, and palm trees whose tops grazed a high glass ceiling.

Although Francie was alone with the man, she could see her friend through the glass. Raven was sitting in another room at a small table with a cup of tea, looking put out.

Francie turned back to the man and got right to the point. "You know something about my mother?" she asked.

"All in good time," the excessively bald man said, wiping his hairless paws on his dressing gown. "I am a collector. Of, as you can see, plants," he added, gesturing unnecessarily to the jungle around him. He smiled, revealing a row of tiny, jewel-like teeth, pearly white, studded here and there with gold.

"I believe we have a mutual interest," he said.

"My mother?" Francie asked.

"Well, yes, that," he said. "But first, something else that you have."

"Something that I have?" She thought of the bookmark and how she had hoped to identify the plant, and she took it out of her pocket. "This?" she asked.

His eyes lit up and he clasped the strip of paper to his heart.

"You recognize it?" she asked.

"Oh, my!" he said. "Oh, my, yes." He stared down at the flower on the bookmark as if at his own newborn baby. "Now come along." He took her arm and guided her along the path through jungle-like foliage.

"Are you going to show me the flower on the bookmark?" she asked.

He chuckled and said, "Right now I'd like to give you a tour. Each room is climate controlled to produce the best results. This section features tropical plants." He waved his hand at the tangle of ferns and huge-leafed trees with variegated leaves. Thick vines wound up the tree trunks, which were also covered with—what were those plants that grew on other plants called? Epiphytes?

She felt sticky under her winter sweater.

A door slid open with a kind of gasp, and they stepped into a vestibule before entering another room, this one less humid.

"Now we are in a more temperate climate with soils to match," he said, pointing at somewhat more familiar-looking plants.

Francie hoped they weren't going to go any farther—Raven had given her a plaintive look as she and the plant man had started moving for the far door—but on they went. Next was the desert room, filled with strange, spiky, or multiarmed cacti and colorful succulents. Francie couldn't help but notice a large saguaro—maybe twenty feet tall with a couple of arms held up as if someone were holding a gun to its head.

"You are admiring my saguaro," he said.

"Not exactly," Francie said. "I was remembering that saguaros are the most frequently stolen plants in the country."

He snorted. "I don't need to steal anything. I have enough money to *buy* what I want." He pointed his shears at a bench and said, "Sit down."

She sat.

"This is the poison room." He laughed.

Francie edged away from the plant that was tickling the back of her neck. "Um," she said. "This has been interesting, but I really don't have permission to be gone—"

"A whole little section devoted to plants from which poisons are derived," the man went on as if she hadn't spoken. "Wolfsbane, yew, nightshade, yellow oleander. This lily"—the man pointed with the tips of his shears—"is toxic to humans. Its pollen can cause vomiting and drowsiness. Even so, the plant also has many medicinal applications."

"I thought you had information about my mother," Francie inserted as assertively as she could.

"In due time," Mr. Baldo said.

"Also," Francie went on, "if I don't get back right away, I'm going to be in trouble with my teacher."

The man just waved her objections away. "I can teach you plenty," he said. "For instance, *Nepenthes attenboroughii*, otherwise known as Attenborough's pitcher plant." He pointed to a bizarre neon green and purple tube-like plant whose blossom yawned open-mouthed. "It's a carnivorous plant that can digest large insects. Even shrews and rats. Perhaps I will try to grow one big enough to swallow a baby."

In reaction to Francie's look of horror, he said, "Of course I'm kidding."

Was he? Francie wasn't sure.

"It's one of the very rarest plants, and I have one. In fact, I have collected all the rarest plants in the world; many of them are growing right here before your eyes. This tree," he went on, gesturing to a large palm tree that seemed to stretch all the way to the glass building's top, "is known as a suicide tree. It grows for fifty years, then creates a cluster of flowers called an inflorescence, after which it dies, committing suicide, if you will."

"This is all very interesting," Francie said. "But—"

Mr. Baldo clucked his tongue and pointed at a yellow and purple blossom. "Rothschild's slipper orchid—one of the rarest flowers in the world—you see how it resembles a slipper. I paid five thousand dollars for a single stem."

"Perhaps the plants are best left in their natural habitat," Francie suggested. "Especially the rare ones."

"Ah, you might think so, but look how well I care for them. Look how I love them! If they are way out in some jungle or another, they might go unloved, even unseen! How sad would that be?"

"I'm not sure the main reason plants exist is to be seen or loved by humans. I think they're likely to be part of some important ecosystem that needs them."

"Oh yes, quite right," Mr. Baldo cooed. "The little tree shrew uses the pitcher plant as a toilet. Where will the little shrew go poo-poo now?"

He turned his gaze lovingly back to the orchid, murmuring, "Only six blooms remain on the one known plant that still exists in the wild. And I have one right here!"

Then he turned to Francie and said, his voice nearly trembling with emotion, "There is still one plant that I don't have. The rarest of the rare. So rare that it is believed to be extinct." He stared intently at Francie. "So rare that the plant itself is, indeed, extinct."

Francie held his gaze, then finally said, "So . . . it's extinct. In other words, does not exist anymore."

"And yet . . ." the man said, pointing to her bookmark, still clasped in her hand. "There's still hope."

"This?" She stared at the bookmark. "You do realize that this is a painting of a plant, not a real plant?"

"You possess a box, a small silver box."

Francie was silent.

"I want it. And you will give it to me."

"Even if I did have a box like you describe, why would I give it to you?"

"Because then I will help you find your mother."

"How?"

He shook his head. "Quid pro quo. That means, I want something from you first."

"I know what quid pro quo means."

"Good, then you understand that once you deliver the box, I help you contact your mother."

He moved toward her, making Francie take a couple of quick steps backwards—right into some sharp prickers. She squelched a yelp. Instead, she said, "And what does a box have to do with an extinct plant?"

He squinted at her and tilted his head. "It seems I know quite a bit more than you do." He tapped the closed shears against the palm of his hand and went on. "Yet another thing I know, and perhaps you suspect, is that there are plenty of people who want to find your mother, and not all of them have her—or your— best interests at heart. If you work with me, I have, as you will have noticed, quite a lot of resources at my disposal. I have ways of finding things—and people—that I want to find."

"Then you can find that box you're looking for without my help."

"That's what we thought, but it seems it's not quite so easy."

"What do you mean . . . ?" Francie said, feeling the revving of her heart, picturing the box inside the microwave, a stupid place to hide something if there ever was one.

"Oh, yes," he said. "While you were absorbing thousands of years of art history, your *quaint*"—he paused to put air quotes around the word—"apartment was quite thoroughly searched. The box was not found."

They forgot to look in the microwave? That's a no-brainer, right? Francie tried to keep her face neutral while her mind whirred. Even a small child would have been able to find the box in her apartment.

"Well, for all our sakes, I hope you can retrieve it," he said. "If not . . . I shudder to think what might happen . . ." The man let out a sigh so heavy, Francie felt the movement of air around her, carrying the scent of exotic plants and expensive cologne.

"Off you go now!" He rang a little bell, clapped his hands, and the chauffeur appeared from behind the rhododendrons. She bowed slightly to Mr. Baldo and then politely to Francie.

"Georgina here will be getting you back to your school chums," Mr. Baldo said. "Oh, and it really would not be in your best interest to mention our visit to anyone. I'm sure you'll be in enough trouble as it is. Ta ta!" His embroidered dressing gown snapped slightly as he turned then stepped into another room. The doors, as he passed through, gasped as if with their dying breath.

On the drive back to their classmates, Raven stared angrily out the window while Francie wondered if she should have told the plant collector that the box was empty. There wasn't anything in it—animal, vegetable, or mineral. But maybe she could get some information about her mother before he discovered that. All she had to do was to get the box to him—if the box was still in her apartment. It was hard to believe that whoever had searched it had not thought to look in the microwave.

The driver dropped them off on the nearest street and told them to walk through the park to the conservatory.

"Are you going to tell me what all that was about?" Raven asked as they walked.

"He is a plant collector," Francie said, showing Raven the card he'd given her. "Reginald P. Skitterly, Esq."

"That cannot be a real name," Raven said.

As they came up the walk and confronted the crowd, Raven said, "Well, no surprise. Everybody's pretty mad." She glared at Francie. "Including me."

Their classmates were mad because they had run out of time to go to a restaurant for dinner and now were going to stop at McDonald's instead. The teachers were beside themselves with worry. Ms. Hanover started weeping when she saw Francie and Raven. Between sobs, she managed to choke out, "Where have you been? What do you have to say for yourself?"

Francie had nothing to say for herself. She hadn't concocted a story, and since anything she could say would lead down a rabbit hole, she said nothing.

Raven stammered out a few sentences about how Francie hadn't felt well and wanted to get some air, and Raven had gone along to make sure she was safe.

"The principal wants to talk to you first thing tomorrow morning," Ms. Hanover said. "Both of you."

Francie and Raven nodded and walked onto and through the bus, past their classmates, whose faces ranged from angry to incredulous to disgusted to, in at least one case, a little admiring.

Jay was sitting in a seat by himself toward the back of the bus. Raven slid in next to him and Francie slid into the seat across from them. The guy who'd had the seat to himself before she arrived scooched as far toward the window as he could manage and made a show of readjusting his earbuds, wordlessly communicating, *Don't talk to me.*

"What the heck?" Jay said, his brows knitted in consternation. "What happened? Did you fall into a Stygian sleep or what?"

That made Francie laugh, for which she was grateful.

"Be glad you missed it," Raven said, slumping in her seat and opening a book. "You don't have to be in the principal's office tomorrow morning."

"Francie? Are you going to tell me what happened?" Jay asked.

But Francie was closemouthed. She'd already endangered her friends enough. It hadn't really dawned on her until today just how serious this was. And how her friends could get swept up into real, serious danger. She was no friend to them if she didn't try to keep them out of it.

So she said nothing, and Raven went back to her book and Jay to his phone, and Francie sat and gnawed on her lunch, as if the cold burger with its wilted lettuce and rubbery cheese was a kind of penance.

Back in Walpurgis late that night, Ms. Hanover reminded Francie and Raven they were due at the office next morning. They nodded and piled into Jay's car.

They rode in silence until Raven said, "It's one thing for you to get into trouble at school, and something else for me."

Francie turned to look at her in the dim light.

"You'll probably get a slap on the wrist. You made a little mistake," Raven said. "But everybody *expects* me to get into trouble. So when I get into trouble, I'm just living up to their expectations. Another thing: your granddad will pay your college tuition. I have to get a scholarship. So I can't mess up!"

"I'm sorry," Francie said. "You should have stayed back! I told you to!"

Jay pulled up in front of Francie's building. "Are you sure you're going to be okay?"

"You can come and stay at my house," Raven mumbled.

Francie smiled at her. "You're even nice when you're mad! Thanks, but I need some time to think. I'll be fine."

"Well, we're going up there with you," Jay said.

"No," Francie said. "Go home. I'll be fine. I've got a lock on the door." She hopped out of the car and dashed up the stairs.

Francie should have been prepared for what she'd find: couch cushions on the floor, the hall table drawer open, the area rug thrown aside. She shuddered. It was a hideous feeling knowing someone had been in your home, gone through all your things. But she walked right past the mess and stepped into the kitchen.

Just about every door and drawer was open: cupboard, oven, closet, bathroom, bedroom, kitchen. Just about the only door that was not open was the microwave. Francie approached it with apprehension, reaching toward it as if it might bite her.

The door swung open. The microwave was empty.

14
A BIT OF DOWN

"Holy breaking and entering!"

Jay's voice came from the front door that Francie had probably forgotten to lock behind her. Had she forgotten to lock it this morning, too?

Raven and Jay found her in the kitchen.

"I am in . . . So. Much. Trouble," she said.

"What's going on?" Raven asked.

"The box," Francie said, collapsing into a chair, "is gone." She stretched her arms out on the table and flung her head down on them. "You should go home, you guys. Go home right now. Don't get mixed up in this."

"We're already mixed up in it," Raven said. "If you will recall, Jay and I said we were all in. But we can't help unless you keep us informed. Where did you put it? The box, I mean."

"In the microwave."

"Are you sure that's where you put it?"

"Yes, of course I'm sure!" Francie snapped. "I'm sorry. I'm just very upset."

"I get that," Raven said. "Any idea who did this?" She spread her arms out to indicate the mess.

Francie wasn't ready to try to explain the whole big weird mess, so she shook her head. "I'm just in so much trouble," Francie said. "School. Granddad. Theo." *And*, she thought but didn't add, *the plant guy who is expecting to get the box.* Francie had no idea what he'd do if he didn't. And she didn't want to find out. Plus the tantalizing promise of finding her mother—that dream went up in a puff of smoke.

"We just have to find the box, that's all," Raven said, as if it were a puppy that would turn up any minute. "Although, are we feeling like it's even that important? I mean, since there's nothing in it and the box isn't very valuable . . ."

"I don't know," Francie said. "Maybe there's still something about it that we don't know."

"What do *you* think, Jay?" Raven said. "Jay?"

Francie looked up. "Where did he go?"

"I'm out here," Jay called from the other room.

Francie and Raven found Jay in the living room, turning over chairs, then turning them upright again. "Whoever it was probably left something behind, right?" he said. "A footprint. A hair."

"Sure, CSI Walpurgis," Raven joked. "You got a DNA lab somewhere?"

"A cigarette butt," Jay said, ignoring her remark. "Something!"

"I think they're professionals. They probably don't leave stuff lying around," Francie said.

"What's this, then?" Raven said, pointing to a tiny feather clinging to the small cactus on the end table. And with the feather the tiniest shred of fabric.

Jay took a Swiss Army knife from his pocket, extracted the

tweezers from its slot, and carefully lifted the shred of cloth from the spines of the cactus.

"Huh!" Francie said. "That cactus is good for something after all."

"Get a magnifying glass," Jay said.

"A magnifying glass?" Francie said. "Who do you think I am, Sherlock Holmes?"

"Never mind," Jay said. He took the bit of fabric back to the kitchen and got a glass from the cupboard. As he was filling it with water he said, "Supposedly this should work like a magnifying glass."

Raven peered through the water in the glass at the piece of cloth and said, "It's a lot like looking through a glass of water at a shred of orange fabric."

"Red," Jay said, peering at it through the glass. "Although it's true this thing does not work."

"It's blaze orange, Jay," Raven said. "Sure of it."

While Jay and Raven had been arguing about the color of the fabric, Francie's mind had been click, click, clicking. If whoever had been working for the plant collector had not found the box, it must have been stolen by someone else. Maybe even someone who lived here, who had heard about it or seen it.

"How many blaze-orange down jackets are there in this town?" Francie asked.

"A lot," Raven said. "But fewer that are shedding down. We'll start snooping in earnest tomorrow."

"We probably should get home. School starts in a few hours," Jay said.

"Come and stay at my house, Frenchy," Raven begged, tugging on her arm.

"No," Francie said. "Whoever it was got what they wanted. I'm sure I'm safe now."

. . . . .

After they were gone, Francie locked the door behind them, walked through the mess, and flung herself on her bed where she fell almost instantly into a deep and troubled, one could even say *Stygian*, sleep.

15

TROUBLE

FRANCIE WOKE JUST MINUTES before she was scheduled to be in the principal's office.

"Well, at least I don't have to take any time to get dressed," she mumbled as she threw her jacket over her sleep-rumpled clothes, then started running the several blocks to school. It was faster than driving and trying to find a place to park.

Her phone rang and she picked up.

"Granddad!" she said, panting, while also trying to use her chipper voice.

"What have you done now?" he hollered, not bothering with a hello. "I got a call from the school telling me you're in trouble." Not waiting for an answer, he rattled on, "Did I not tell you you were grounded and not allowed to go on that field trip? And also you misrepresented it as something else. You said 'feed drip' or some such."

"No, you misheard what I said. You told me to go to school, and I did—my class happened to go on a *field trip*." That's all she could come up with. She'd only been awake for a few minutes and had not yet achieved full mental strength.

"Young lady, you are not to go anywhere or do anything until we get there. Theo's making the arrangements."

"What?" Francie pushed through the doors of the school. "When—?"

Theo's voice came on the phone. "Granddad wants us to come home to see what's going on with you."

"No!" Francie yelped, perhaps a little too forcefully. "I mean, that's not necessary. It's not that big a deal. I can explain later."

"Well, we're on our way to the airport now."

Thanks a lot, Francie thought. *Now in lieu of breakfast I have that information to digest.*

"You're late," the principal said, ushering her into his office.

Ms. Hanover was there already, wearing a crisp white blouse and a sour expression. Raven was there, too, looking down at her shoes.

Francie glanced around at the others: the principal, leaning against his desk. A policeman lurking in the corner. A policeman? Was that really necessary? Ms. Hanover eyed Francie's slept-in clothes and general dishevelment, then gave Francie a concerned look before asking, "Do you have an explanation for your behavior yesterday?"

"First of all," Francie said, "let me just say that Raven only went with me to keep me out of trouble."

"Well, she didn't succeed," the principal said, "and she got herself into trouble, too."

"Seriously, it was all my fault. Raven tried to get me to come back, but I wouldn't. She was trying to do the right thing; she doesn't deserve punishment."

Ms. Hanover looked them both over, then said, "I believe her. It would be like Raven to try to protect her friend."

"Fine," the principal said. "Raven, you can go."

Raven's face registered surprise, and she got up, glanced back at Francie, and left the office.

Not knowing where to look, Francie turned her gaze to the window behind the principal's desk. Students streamed by, sliced into ribbons by the slatted blinds. The scene reminded her of a piece she'd seen in the modern art section of the museum the day before.

Ms. Hanover recounted Francie's transgressions to the principal: "Drifted away from the group . . . didn't do the assignment . . . avoided her friends . . ." while Francie wondered how she was ever going to find the box with only a shred of fabric and a tiny white feather as clues.

Francie had to get that box back before Theo and Granddad showed up. She couldn't face Theo if she lost the box. Plus there was the plant collector's promise to find her mother if she delivered it to him.

". . . belligerent . . . ill-behaved . . . set a bad example . . . ," Ms. Hanover was saying.

She was already in enough trouble with Granddad.

". . . always thought of Francesca as a good student, but now . . ."

Miss Hanover trailed off and Francie looked up. Her teacher's face had turned blotchy and red. "I'm just so disappointed!" she cried.

Francie tried to look remorseful, while her mind whizzed. Say Theo and Granddad left New York at 8 a.m. Then there was a three-hour flight. Layover, maybe another hour. Another flight, one hour. Getting to and from the airport . . .

"I mean, I had been wooing her to play the lead in the

upcoming play, and, well, now I'm glad she said no!" Ms. Hanover sputtered.

"Six hours," Francie muttered.

"Excuse me?" Ms. Hanover said.

"So sorry," Francie said, hanging her head. "I said, 'I'm so sorry.'" She meant to go on, but something had caught her eye. Something on the floor by her feet: a feather. A small downy feather like the one that had been stuck to her cactus.

Francie glanced at Ms. Hanover. Any feathers on her? No. Anyway, it couldn't be her. She'd been on the field trip. The principal? He of the folded arms and knitted brow? She thought not. Policeman? No.

The principal had taken over for Ms. Hanover, continuing to recount Francie's sins: "Left the building . . . expressly told not to do so . . . gone for nearly an hour . . . didn't tell anyone where you were going . . ."

Francie mumbled, "I'm sorry," every now and then when it seemed like it might be appropriate. She had six hours to find out who stole the box and to get it back. An insurmountable task. Like one of the tasks Psyche had to accomplish to win back Cupid: sorting wheat and poppy seeds and lentils, gathering wool from a flock of murderous sheep, retrieving a box of beauty from the underworld.

The thought made her turn her head away from the whole situation. When she did, she could see through the glass door separating the principal's office from the area where the secretaries held forth.

One scrawny middle-schooler stood at the reception desk. Another person sat in one of the rows of chairs along the wall, but all she could see of this person were his legs, sticking straight out into the corridor in a belligerent way.

None of that mattered to Francie. What her eye settled on was the incongruously dainty feather clinging to the pant leg of one of those legs.

"Francesca!" the principal barked. "Are you even listening to what we say?"

Francie's head rotated back to him, but not before she glimpsed the belligerent legs standing up and walking out of the office, and then—the legs were gone!

"Francesca?"

She looked up.

"Isn't there something you'd like to say?"

They were probably looking for some sort of explanation, so she concocted a story about how she'd left the conservatory and Raven had followed, begging her to come back, but she wouldn't, and then they had gotten lost and didn't have their phones, so it had taken them quite a while to find their way back. Rather than looking directly at her audience, she gazed just past them, through the slatted blinds.

Following her explanation, she started in on a heartfelt apology. "I can't tell you how sorry I am," she began, noticing that the earlier color and movement beyond the blinds were gone—all the students now in their appointed classes. "I can honestly say it won't happen again, and . . ." Between the slats were just snowy white wedges, like a coconut layer cake—except, there! A slice of orange! Someone walking by. Someone whose jacket was ribboned into sections of blaze orange. And a pair of belligerent-looking legs striding away.

". . . and so I offer my sincerest apologies," Francie finished.

The principal excused her to go to her first-hour class and told her to report back after school for detention. As she left the office, she heard the policeman say, "Too bad. She seemed like she was quite the little Nancy Drew there for a while."

· · · · ·

Even though she knew that she was not improving her situation at school by cutting class, Francie slipped out a side door, dashed across the parking lot, and started off in the direction of the orange jacket. She couldn't just let it go by and not figure out who was inside of it.

It didn't take long to spy the jacket-wearing figure walking down the hill toward the two blocks of what constituted downtown.

She followed at a distance and watched as whoever it was went into the Sportsman's Café. *Okay,* Francie thought, *there are worse places to go when you haven't had breakfast.*

She opened the door of the café and stepped into an eye-blistering blaze of orange. Blaze-orange caps, pants, shirts, and jackets were everywhere—draped over chairs or hung from hooks on the ends of booths. Some were being worn. She might have stepped into some kind of bizarre fashion shoot, with models a bit on the grizzled and paunchy side. But of course it was not that. It was just a bunch of hunters having breakfast before hitting their deer stands.

She wasn't sure if the figure she'd followed at a distance was still here or not, so she slowly made her way around the room, trying to inspect jackets without being too weird about it, looking for bits of fluffy down leaking from a tear in a sleeve, perhaps. Then, cutting through the hazy smoke of grilling bacon and hash browns, she heard a familiar voice. In fact, it was the very same voice she had heard when she and Raven had been hidden in the ramshackle cabin closet. And now she could make out the form of the person she had been following, threading his way through the throng to the back of the restaurant. It was someone she knew, someone she'd had dealings with in the past, her classmate Buck Thorne Jr.

She wove among the tables toward him, trying—and failing, no doubt—to not look awkward, and managing to catch a few phrases before he disappeared out the back door.

Francie started after him, but a whole booth's worth of guys slid out and stood up, blocking the way to the back door. By the time Francie got around them and outside, Buck was already in his truck. All she could do was stand and watch as he drove away.

Feeling deflated, she checked her phone. There was just enough time to get a coffee and still make it back to school in time for biology. While waiting at the counter for her coffee-to-go, she couldn't help overhearing the conversation behind her.

"Poor Buck," cooed somebody. Francie turned to see a young woman in a blaze-orange flannel shirt, sipping from a mug. "What's up with him?" the young woman said. "How come he's not hunting?"

"Community service!" someone else laughed. "He got caught cutting spruce tops without a permit on public land."

More laughter.

"What's he doing, then?"

"For community service? Working at the municipal skating rink, helping the kiddies with their skates."

Francie addressed the young woman. "Would he be there now?" she asked.

The woman shrugged and said, "Probably not yet. I think there are skating lessons for preschoolers after school."

Well, bingo, Francie thought, plunking down the cash for her coffee and heading back to school.

Third-hour biology. She put her elbow on the desk, propped her head up with her hand, and focused her eyeballs on the front of the class. Normally Mr. Blondeau was pretty interesting, but today she couldn't concentrate, her mind a miasma of questions. *Did Buck steal the box? If he did, why? How could she find that out?*

*Would it be worth chasing him down at the skating rink? Why did
the plant collector think the box had something to do with plants? She
got the feeling he believed there was something inside. Like a plant.
But could a plant survive inside a box? Wouldn't it just disintegrate
or something?*

She was absorbed in these thoughts until the words "five
hundred years . . . lotus seeds sprouted," came out of Mr.
Blondeau's mouth.

"What?" she said out loud.

"I'm sorry, Francesca," Mr. Blondeau said. "Are you having
trouble hearing? Perhaps you should come up to the front."

"I mean did you just say that a five-hundred-year-old seed
sprouted?"

"Yes, several, actually. A number of ancient seeds were recovered from a dry lake bed in China and were successfully
germinated. But that's not the oldest, by any means. In Israel a
date palm was grown from a two-thousand-year-old seed. Okay,
but that's still not the oldest. The oldest seed that's ever been
sprouted—how old do you think it is? Anybody? Anybody?"
Mr. Blondeau shoved his glasses up on his nose, hitched up his
pants, and bounced on his toes, as he did whenever he got excited about anything.

"Five thousand years?" someone offered.

"Ten thousand years?" called out someone else.

"No," Mr. Blondeau said. "The oldest regenerated seeds were
found in Siberia and could be as much as thirty-two thousand
years old."

"How could seeds stay viable all that time?" Jay asked.

There was some slight teasing from the back row about the
word *viable*. "How do you stay viable, Jay?" "*Viable* is Jay's middle
name." And so on.

"It's a perfectly valid question," Mr. Blondeau said, cutting off the jokesters. "And the answer is that the seeds were entirely encased in ice more than a hundred feet below the permafrost. They were found surrounded by layers of mammoth, bison, and woolly rhinoceros bones."

"So those seeds were kept frozen, but not the ones in Israel," Francie said. "Israel doesn't have permafrost. Does that mean that seeds can stay alive for a long time in any kind of condition?"

"Not any kind. In the case of the Siberian plant, those seeds were found 124 feet below permafrost—so they were frozen. The date palm seeds were discovered in very dry desert soil, which probably preserved them, and the lotus seeds also in a dry lake bed. So, yes, different kinds of conditions, but nonetheless conditions in which a seed could be preserved."

I wonder, Francie thought, sinking back into her seat. *The plant collector had hinted that the box had something to do with a plant believed to be extinct. In fact, according to him, the plant itself was extinct, but then he had added, "There's still hope." Could the "hope" be that seeds of this plant still existed? Could it be that what had been inside the box were seeds?*

16
THE STAKEOUT

"I BET NOT VERY MANY DETECTIVES do stakeouts of ice-skating rinks," Raven said.

Francie and Raven sipped hot coffee in paper cups while sitting in Francie's car in the parking lot and stared out at the frozen lake. A small rink had been cleared of snow and was crowded with snowsuit-swaddled preschoolers clinging to their parents' hands or pushing tiny chairs around. The warming shack door opened and closed, opened and closed, as skaters went in and out.

"Is every town around here situated on the shores of a lake?" Francie asked.

"Pretty much," Raven answered, rattling around in the paper bag of donuts. "What would be the point in existing otherwise?"

"So, every town has its lake and every town also has a giant something?" Francie said. "Like Walpurgis has its giant muskie."

"There are a couple of Paul Bunyans," Raven said.

"His giant sweetheart, his giant cradle," Francie added.

"A gigantic hockey stick, the world's biggest ball of twine..."

They stopped to watch a bunch of kids get into a tussle, with one boy shoving another little boy into a snowbank and others piling on top of him.

Francie and Raven were about to go rescue the kid when the warming shack door was flung open and out charged an orange-jacketed figure who slid and skittered across the ice rink toward the fracas.

"That's Buck!" Raven said.

He yanked the kids off the pile and tossed them onto the rink, one by one. He shook his finger at the offenders and turned to the little boy who was swiping at his face with his wet mittens. Francie and Raven leaned forward, wondering if the boy was about to get a scolding or what. Buck picked up the crying kid, set him upright on the ice, brushed the snow off him, and patted him on the head, then slid across the ice, clearly giving the bullies a warning as he went by. Francie's opinion of Buck softened somewhat—but even from here she could see the square of silver duct tape on the sleeve of his blaze-orange jacket.

Francie and Raven got out of the car and walked toward the ice, intending to go have a chat with him. But at the shore's edge, Francie stopped dead. Froze. The periphery of her vision went fuzzy and dark at the memory of breaking through the ice, the plunge into frigid water. Tiny bright stars twinkled in front of her eyes, and she felt not warm blood but ice water coursing through her veins. She found herself unable to move, except for some very violent trembling.

Raven turned back. "You okay?"

"I just... I guess I wasn't prepared for how I'd feel being on ice again," Francie said.

"Right," Raven agreed. "Listen, why don't you wait in the warming shack and I'll go talk to Buck?"

"Okay," Francie said weakly, feeling so faint with fear she had to sit down. Raven guided her inside and across the warming house floor, pulpy from being hacked up by skate blades. She sat Francie down on a bench also softened by skate blades and carved initials.

"I'll be back soon," Raven promised.

Francie felt foolish. What was wrong with her? Look at these five-year-olds clomping in and out of the warming house with their double-bladed skates! And here she sat trembling on a bench in the corner, too afraid to even go outside!

A man came in, passed by Francie, turned back, and stopped. "Are you all right?" he asked softly. "Everything okay?" He had the kind of chiseled handsome face of a movie actor, like the rugged, somewhat worse-for-wear hero of an old Western.

Francie nodded. Afraid she might burst into tears, she didn't trust herself to say anything.

He continued past but swiveled his head to take another look at her.

She offered him a wan smile. Unlike the other parka-and-jeans-wearing parents coming and going, he was wearing an expensive-looking topcoat, and expensive-looking slacks and a pair of brand-new leather boots. He seemed out of place in this beat-up shack with its graffiti-covered walls and carved-up benches.

"Haven't got used to dressing for this weather," he said, rubbing his leather-gloved hands together.

She almost suggested he wear mittens instead of gloves, something she'd had to learn herself, but thought better of it. Instead she said, "Are you . . . skating?"

"Haha!" he chortled. "No. My daughter is." He pointed in the direction of the rink. "I just came in to warm up. How about you?" he asked her. Obviously, she didn't have skates either.

"I'm just waiting for someone," she said, also pointing toward the rink.

"Well, if you need any help or anything—I mean, if I can be of service . . . ," he said, reaching into his jacket as if he were about to get something to give her.

But she didn't find out what because just then Raven stuck her head in the door, said, "Francie!" and gestured to her to come outside.

Francie said, "Sorry, gotta go," and got up and went out the door.

"I didn't think you'd want to talk to Buck in there," Raven said, nodding at the warming house.

"You're right," Francie said, swiveling her head to give the shack a glance and wondering if that guy was some kind of health professional or what. Why had he wanted to help her? But now there was Buck to deal with, and that was far more urgent. He looked supremely uncomfortable while at the same time put out, especially since Raven had taken hold of his sleeve as if he might dart away at any moment.

"Where is it?" Francie asked him.

"Where is what?" Buck said.

"You know what I'm talking about. What you stole from my apartment."

"I don't know what you're talking about."

"I think you do," Francie reached over and pulled a little feather from under the flap of duct tape on his sleeve.

"Hey!" he protested.

"I'll call the cops," Francie said, "unless you give that box back to me."

"I don't have it," he said. His shoulders slumped. The constant smirk he wore was gone.

So he did take the box, Francie realized. She was almost

surprised to discover that. But she didn't let on, asking him coolly, "Where is the box now?"

"I gave it to someone."

"To whom?" Francie said.

"Whom?" Buck looked confused.

"She means, who did you give it to, you dumb schnitzel," Raven said. "I'm gonna shake you 'til your teeth come out your back end if you don't hurry up and offer some useful information." Raven put her hands on his shoulders and gave him a little warning shake.

"Okay, okay!" he whined. "Don't have a cat fit. I gave it to that lady at the museum. She said there was a gentleman who might want to buy it."

"Wait now, what? Did she tell you to steal it from me?" Francie asked.

"Not exactly," he said.

"What does 'not exactly' mean?"

"She might have hinted . . . but mostly I did it to get back at you for ratting me out."

"What?"

"To the DNR. About cutting trees and stuff," Buck said. "I mean, I just figured it had to be you. You're the detective, right?"

"Are you kidding me?" Francie said. "You did it just to get back at me? Why'd you take that, though? Out of everything at my place, why the box?"

"I figured it must be the most valuable thing you had since you kept it in the microwave. I mean, that's where I keep valuable things—because you have to open it in order to use it, right?—so you're not going to forget and preheat it like that one time I preheated the oven for a frozen pizza but forgot I'd put a wad of cash in there."

"You broke into my apartment to do that?"

"Broke in? No! Your door was open. I actually went in there to see if something was wrong. Then I remembered the whole art class was gone on a field trip. And, well, as long as I was in there, I decided to check the microwave."

"So the box is at the museum?" Francie said.

Buck shrugged. "I suppose. Unless she sold it already. Are you going to call the cops?"

"I should," Francie said, walking away. "But I'm not. But you owe me."

She was suddenly aware that the man she'd talked to in the warming shack was standing not very far away. Had he been eavesdropping? Or was she being paranoid?

When she cast an angry glance his way, he pointed to the swarm of tots stumbling around on the rink. "That's my daughter," he said. "In the pink. Nice job, Kylie!" he called and waved. "I have to go now. Bye! Your mom will pick you up."

Apparently the little girl in the pink couldn't hear him. She didn't wave back, and the man walked, jingling his car keys, toward the parking lot.

"Next stop, the museum," Francie said to Raven, heading to her car.

"I gotta go take my grandma to the doctor," Raven said.

"What's wrong?" Francie said.

"She tries to ration out her insulin. Because it costs too much. Then she gets sick."

"Geez, I'm sorry," Francie said. "And I'm really sorry about getting you into trouble."

"Can you just give me a lift so I can pick up my mom's car? Mom's working, so I said I'd take Grandma."

"Sure," Francie said. "Hop in."

"And then when I get back, I'll go to the museum with you," Raven said, buckling her seat belt.

Francie pulled the car out of the lot and headed toward Raven's house. "That's okay," she said. "I can go by myself."

"We can do it later, Frenchy," Raven said. "Or tomorrow. The museum's not going anywhere."

"I have to do it now!" Francie insisted. "Before Theo gets here."

"I don't want you doing dangerous stuff by yourself," Raven said.

"Good grief!" Francie said. "It's the county historical museum! It's not like they're running a drug cartel or anything. I'll be fine."

After dropping Raven off, Francie drove back to the museum and parked in the small lot behind the building. Then she walked around to the front door, which was slightly ajar—odd, given how cold it was. Snow had drifted in through the crack in the door.

"Hello?" she said softly.

What was the chance she'd be alone in the museum, she wondered as she stepped inside. After all that bright sun on white snow, her eyes needed time to adjust to the much dimmer light. But so far it seemed she was alone. That would give her the opportunity to scrounge around for the box without having to confront that snappish museum lady.

Where would the box be, she wondered. Inside a display case? On top of a case? In the office in a drawer? In a safe? It was, after all, stolen. It wouldn't just be on display, would it?

On the other hand, she couldn't rule out the possibility that it could be hiding in plain sight, right? I mean, who would notice if it were among the ladies' jewelry boxes here? Among the curiosities in this cabinet? Or here, alongside a silver-and-ivory brush and comb set?

But it was not in any of those places, and she moved through the museum, gazing into the cases as if into crystal balls, working her way from front to back.

Her phone dinged. She pulled it out of her pocket and groaned when she saw the text from Theo: *At airport, renting car. Be there 30–45 min.*

She pulled off her mittens and texted a thumbs-up, though she felt entirely thumbs-down about it.

Beating back a feeling of panic, she clutched her mittens and phone as she continued toward the back of the building. Her eyes scanned the baskets, bowls, utensils, shaving tools, old household items, and beaded moccasins. In this way she made her way toward the gloomy recesses where the animals were displayed: taxidermied porcupines, baby bear cubs climbing a tree, a snarling bobcat who'd seen better days. The large display case against the back wall was filled with a number of water fowl, including a blue heron who stared down into a one-dimensional painted pond, a duck sitting on a nest of sticks and twigs, and a Canada goose, its long neck craned as if looking for someone. None of them seemed overly concerned about the large black bear looming on his hind legs behind them all.

It was strange, she thought, to see these unmoving creatures. Over the past summer, at her great-aunts' cabin, she'd observed wild creatures and their wild ways. One thing she had learned watching them was that, with few exceptions, they were hardly ever still. If you wanted to see animals in the forest, you watched for movement. Seeing them here, inanimate, behind glass, their iridescent feathers and lustrous fur dulled by dust and death, and their bright, quick eyes replaced with staring glass, it was unnatural—and creepy. Especially creepy that many of them seemed to be staring straight at her. So much so that she found herself keeping an eye on the animals in case any of them decided to make a move.

That's why she didn't see the obstacle in her path—a fairly major obstacle—and why, when she tripped over it, she went sprawling, her phone clattering on the tile floor and her breath knocked clean out of her.

She was getting to her knees when something inside the large display case caught her eye. In the nest. Under the duck. Something she wouldn't have noticed if she weren't on her hands and knees. Something shiny and silver.

She clutched her throat, trying to get a breath. Could it be? She crawled toward it. Yes! In the nest, tucked under the duck as if it were a precious egg, was the silver box.

All she had to do was get inside that big case. She pushed herself up, pausing to glance back to see what had tripped her. If she'd had any breath left in her lungs, she would have screamed. Sprawled on the floor behind Francie was the museum lady, who looked very much not alive. Which is to say she looked dead. Near the woman's head, in a pool of blood, lay a familiar stone knife.

17
MORE TROUBLE

FRANCIE BACKED AWAY, scooted around the museum lady's prone body, and shot out of the building. After a dash to the parking lot, she climbed into her car and sat, trying to take deep, calming breaths, but mostly getting the hyperventilating kind.

"Breathe," she instructed herself. "Calm down. Think."

Outside the car, the sun was blazing, setting the snow alight with eye-piercing whiteness. Inside the car, her mind was a snowstorm—a howling blizzard of thoughts—each thought in opposition to the next.

Call the police.

Don't call the police.

Get out of here!

Go back and get the box.

What if the murderer is still in there?

Her heart was beating so hard she had to press her hands against her chest.

No, the right thing to do was to call the police. Yes, that was the thing she had to do. Right now.

She reached into her jacket pocket. Tried the other pocket. No phone. Patted her jeans, looked around the car, dug in her backpack. Looked at her hands—bare. Her mittens. Where were her mittens? Inside. With her phone. Both of which had flown from her hands when she fell.

She had to go back in there and get her phone. So she could call the police. Yes, that was what she had to do.

With cold hands and thudding heart, Francie went back inside. Just to get her phone, she told herself. Moving through the museum aisles, she thought it through. She'd call, and then the police would come. And then they'd seal the place off as a crime scene. Then she'd never get the box back. Unless . . . unless, she *stole* it back right now.

As she approached the spot where she'd fallen, she told herself that taking the box wasn't stealing, not really, since the box was hers to begin with . . . wasn't it?

When she came to the body, she came to a full stop. Her eyes widened.

The body had moved. And then it groaned.

Oh for the love of Mike! Francie thought, bending down over the lady. *She is alive!*

"Ma'am," she whispered, touching the woman's shoulder. She didn't dare speak louder, because what if the assailant was still in here?

She reached for her phone to call 911 but stopped at the sound of creaking floorboards. Someone was inside the building. Someone who was walking toward her.

In order to reach the phone she would have to move. If she moved, her crinkly down jacket would make noise. Would she be able to pick up the phone without revealing herself?

The knife was closer. Slowly, quietly, she reached toward it but froze when she heard the distinctive crackle of a police radio and a familiar woman's voice speaking to someone over the static: Sheriff Warner.

Forty-five minutes later, Francie found herself in an unenviable spot: in the sheriff's office, surrounded by the sheriff, Theo, the principal, and her granddad, his arm in a sling.

Could she be in any more trouble?

She was truant, as the principal reminded her.

Disobedient, as her grandfather reminded her.

And, according to Theo, mumbling under his breath, she was just plain stupid.

As far as the sheriff was concerned, there were a lot of questions to be answered and her fingerprints to be taken. "Standard procedure," Sheriff Warner assured Francie, tucking a lock of her auburn hair behind an ear. Half-jokingly, she added, with one penciled eyebrow raised, "I'm surprised we don't have them already."

When the sheriff had arrived at the museum, an ambulance was called. Then Francie and the sheriff opened the door to the office to find no one there—only a lot of cold air coming from the open back door.

"The assailant must have escaped out this way," Francie said, trying to sound smart and self-assured. "After he clonked the lady on the head with the knife handle."

"Thank you, little Miss Nancy Drew," Sheriff Warner said. Francie could hear the eye roll in the tone of voice.

After that she kept her thoughts to herself. At least until later, when she was seated in the sheriff's office surrounded by the people with whom she was in trouble. In fact, she was in so much trouble—with everybody—the only way she could cope was to pretend that all this was not really happening. No, it was

just a little play, in which she was a character. A character in a
cop show.

SHERIFF: What were you doing in the museum?
FRANCIE: Looking for something.
SHERIFF: What was that?
FRANCIE: My mittens.

(*So many eyebrows go up you can hear the rustle of eyebrow hair.*)

SHERIFF: How did you get into the museum?
FRANCIE: The door was open.
SHERIFF: When did you leave your mittens at the
museum?
FRANCIE: A few days ago.
SHERIFF: And you just today decided it was so urgent
that you left school to get them.
FRANCIE: My hands were cold. And it was after school.

(*Imaginary chorus, in background, singing*) She's making
it up! She's making it up as she goes!

SHERIFF: So, last week when you left them there—why
did you go that time?
FRANCIE: I went, you know, to look at things. As one
does when one goes to a museum.
SHERIFF: When you were there before, did you talk to
or see Miss Schell?
FRANCIE: Michelle?
SHERIFF: (*spacing the words out*) Miss Schell. The victim.
FRANCIE: How is she?
SHERIFF: Well, she's still alive, but we haven't been
able to talk to her yet. Did you talk to her when you
saw her earlier?

FRANCIE: Briefly. My friends and I were talking to, um, Mr. T.—the other curator. The two of them got in a kind of argument so we left.

SHERIFF: Argument? What about?

FRANCIE: Oh, I mean, I'm sure it wasn't anything serious! I'm not suggesting Mr. T. had anything to do with what happened to Miss Schell. That is, I don't think so . . .

The sheriff asked a host of other questions, almost all of which Francie was able to answer truthfully, as long as she just didn't mention the box. She knew that once they questioned Mr. T. he might mention it, but she'd cross that bridge when it came along. There was too much at stake to bring up the box. For one thing, Theo would kill her if he found out she had shown the box to anyone and then lost track of it. And Mr. Baldo-Skitterly, Esq. had promised to find her mother if she delivered it to him. So whether it had any value or not, she needed it! She had to figure out a way to get into the museum and into that case and extract the box—without anyone knowing about it. Somehow.

Finally, after the grilling, it was just Theo, Granddad, and Francie on the street, walking to Vi's Café for more grilling. Theo held Granddad's good arm, helping him along.

"Well, young lady," Granddad said, "you sure have managed to get yourself into a heap of trouble. Your brother's barely been gone for a few days . . ."

"Oh, I'm pretty sure she could have managed to get into just as much trouble if I'd been here," Theo put in.

"That's true," Francie agreed. "Undeniable."

"Nonetheless, you disobeyed me. And what was all that fuss about you running away yesterday?"

The door jingled as they entered the café, and the grilling resumed almost as soon as they were seated in one of the booths.

Francie sat on one side, Granddad and Theo on the other. Vi approached with a handful of menus and dispensed them to the three silent customers. Turning away from Theo and Granddad, she mouthed, "Uh oh" to Francie.

As soon as Vi was gone, Granddad started the cross-examination.

> GRANDDAD: What kind of trouble *haven't* you gotten
> into? Cutting class, stumbling about in a museum
> full of unconscious bodies?
> FRANCIE: One. One unconscious body.
> GRANDDAD: (*not missing a beat*) In trouble at school—
> you were grounded yet you ran off to Minneapolis!
> FRANCIE: I didn't run off! It was a field trip. For school.
> GRANDDAD: Then you disappear for hours and get into
> trouble with your teachers—
> FRANCIE: I was—
> GRANDDAD: *Wandering* the city streets.
> FRANCIE: I was not wandering—

They all go quiet as Vi returns with three glasses of water and after a glance turns and leaves without asking if they are ready to order.

> FRANCIE: I ended up at this weird dude's conservatory
> where he's growing all these rare plants.
> GRANDDAD: (*turning up his hearing aid*) Go on . . .
> FRANCIE: He told me to get the box—
> GRANDDAD: Pox? What's this about the pox?
> FRANCIE AND THEO: (*a little too loudly*) Box!
> THEO: So you gave the guy the box?
> FRANCIE: No! No, I didn't.

Theo looks relieved. Granddad looks confused.

GRANDDAD: You gave someone the pox?
THEO: (*ignoring him*) Where is it now—the box?

"I'll just go get it," Francie said. "You both stay here. I'll be back in a jiff." When she saw Theo getting up as if to go with her, she waved at him to sit down and added, "A nano-jiff. Won't take a sec."

Francie left the café, glanced both ways as if she were in a spy movie, then plunged down the street toward the museum. What was the chance, she wondered, that she could get in and that she'd be alone in the museum—occupied by neither police nor assailant with murderous intent?

The police were gone when she got there. And the front door was locked. But the back door, miraculously, wasn't. Once inside, it didn't take long to find a big ring of keys dangling from a hook inside the office door. After trying several, Francie found the one that worked on the large glassed-in display case at the back of the museum.

Francie crawled through the small doorway and scuttled around a stand of cattails that shielded the display from the doorway. When she looked up, she stopped in her tracks. The animals, including a large black bear on its hind legs, a bobcat, and a skunk, all faced away from her, giving the impression of momentarily distracted wild creatures, who, once they heard her behind them would turn, see her, be irritated, and, after so long without food, would probably be very hungry.

Francie crawled along, apologizing to the creatures she passed, the bear, the bobcat, the skunk, the blue heron, until she arrived at the duck's nest.

"Pardon me," she whispered as she lifted the duck up and plucked the box from the nest. Just as if it were an egg, she thought, in which lies the giant's heart. What an odd place to hide it—you'd think there'd be a million better places in a museum.

But what if it was a clue from her mother? What if it had been her mother who had knocked poor Miss Schell on the noggin and practically killed her? That would be what Francie had always feared—that her mother was a criminal, and because her mother was a criminal, Francie was doomed to be one, too. Well, here she was, stealing something from a museum, and probably tampering with a crime scene, and who knows what other crimes she was committing. Apparently, she *was* a criminal.

She was just replacing the duck on its nest when she sensed something: it wasn't so much a noise as the kind of vacuum-sucking sound one hears when a door opens somewhere.

Holy crap, she thought, and scurried on her hands and knees past the blue heron, around the bobcat, and behind the bear. The door was still out of reach when she realized that someone was moving about in the office. Not knowing quite where to hide, she dove behind the cattails.

How long would she have to stay here, she wondered? And why, oh why had she chosen this unsustainable position?

She crouched behind the cattails, as unmoving as a taxidermied field mouse. Someone was walking quickly back and forth among the display cases, as if looking for something. Through the glass, Francie could barely hear the faint sound of shoes scuffling against the tile floor, as whoever it was disappeared back into the office behind the display case.

As if she weren't frightened already, it dawned on her that whoever it was might be looking for the box. And whoever that was might be the assailant. Every hair on her head, arms, and unshaved legs stood up as the door behind her creaked open.

18
A SUSPICIOUS DEATH

"FOR THE LOVE OF PETE!" she yelped, turning to see Theo standing in the doorway, hands on hips. "Did you have to scare the living daylights out of me like that?"

"Did you think I couldn't see you hunkered down behind the cattails? You don't exactly blend in, you know, with those hot pink mittens and matching hat."

Francie looked down at the fuzzy pink mittens. "Astrid made them for me," she protested.

"Come on, let's get out of here. You can explain what you were just doing on the way."

"On the way to where?" Francie asked.

"Hurry up!" Theo urged.

Granddad was already sitting in the front seat and Theo got into the driver's seat. That left the back seat for Francie, and she slid inside and set the box on the seat next to her.

"Got it!" she said, triumphantly.

"Can you explain why the box was being displayed in the museum?" Granddad asked as Theo pulled the car out of the lot.

"It wasn't on display," Francie explained. "It was hidden in a duck's nest. You couldn't even see it unless you were on the floor—like I was after I tripped over Miss Schell."

"All right," Granddad said in a measured tone, somewhat forced. "Why was it hidden in a duck's nest?"

"I don't know!" Francie said.

"You didn't put it there?"

"No! Why would I do that?"

"Then how did it get there?"

"I don't know!"

In order to look at her, Granddad had to turn his whole upper torso, which he did. "I'll take that," Granddad said, pointing with his good arm at the box.

Reluctantly, Francie handed it to her grandfather. Then she dug in her pocket to find the plant collector's business card. "Okay, now all we have to do is get in touch with this guy." She pulled out Skitterly's card and handed it to her grandfather. "He said he would help find Mom if I could deliver the box to him. But he only gave me thirty-six hours, so . . ."

"You're just going to hand over the box to some dude?" Theo protested from the driver's seat.

"He's not some dude," Francie said. "He's really rich. He has a lot of connections."

"Okay, so a rich dude, then," Theo said. "That makes it better?"

Francie held the card out to Granddad. "This is the guy," she said.

With his good hand, Granddad slid his glasses out of his pocket, slipped them on, then took the card. "I don't think so," he said, handing the card back to Francie.

"What do you mean, 'You don't think so'?" she cried. "He

said he would help find Mom. He has all the resources at his disposal, et cetera. There's no reason not to give him the box that he thinks is so precious—it's empty, and the box itself is not worth that much. But if he helps us find Mom . . ."

Granddad held up his newspaper for Francie to see.

"What's this?" she said.

He pointed one of his long, authoritative fingers at a photograph and accompanying article.

"That's him!" she gasped. "That's the guy! Reginald Skitterly or whatever."

The headline under the photograph read, "RARE PLANT COLLECTOR FOUND DEAD."

"Dead!" she cried, snatching the newspaper out of Granddad's hands. Skimming the rest of the article, she read, "Reginald Skitterly . . . collected rare plants from around the world . . . including poisonous . . . . possibly poisoned by contact . . . awaiting autopsy results."

She looked up. "I just saw him yesterday! He was fine."

"I don't like it," Granddad said. "Not at all. Not at all."

"Me neither," Francie said, flinging herself back in the seat.

"Everywhere *she* goes"—Granddad's long finger pointed at Francie—"people are knocked unconscious or flat-out murdered. Like that poor fellow Skitterly."

Francie sat bolt upright in the seat. "Wait a minute. What? What's this about murdered?" Francie's eyes went back to the article. "It didn't say he was murdered! It sounded like one of his plants killed him."

"You don't just keel over dead by tending a plant!" Granddad said.

Francie slumped again. This was a crushing blow. It seemed that she had been getting close, maybe, to finding her mother, and the box was going to help in the quest, maybe not in the way she'd imagined, but still. She was quiet, absorbing this, and into her mind came the little chant, the thing she used to whisper to herself as a child late at night to calm herself in the dark before sleep came: *Far, far away there is a lake. In the lake there is an island. On the island is a church, in the church there is a well. . . . A well.* What was it Raven had said about a well? A well is deep. A well represents depths unknown. . . . What if . . . what if there was more to the box than they'd found so far?

She needed to see the box.

As the car rolled to a stop, Francie looked out to see that they had pulled up in front of the regional airport. "Are you going home already, Granddad?" Francie asked, trying not to sound as hopeful as she was.

"No," he said.

"Is Theo going somewhere?" she asked, looking at Theo's reflection in the rearview mirror. He glanced at her, then looked quickly away.

"No," Granddad said. "You are."

"Me?" Francie said. "Why? Where?"

"When you start getting involved in murder and attempted murder, it's time to send you away."

"Wait a minute. I'm not involved in either one of those things."

"The sheriff tells me your fingerprints are all over the weapon used to assault poor Miss Schell." Granddad turned stiffly to face Francie in the back seat. "Yours. Why?"

"You're not seriously accusing me, are you?" Francie said.

"I just want to know how your fingerprints got there. Did you tamper with the crime scene?"

"No!" Francie said. "Of course not. I mean, other than the, you know, the box. Speaking of which," she added, reaching over the seat, "can I see it?"

"No," Granddad said, slapping her hand away. "You'd better explain how your fingerprints got on the murder weapon."

Francie told him about going to the museum and how she and her friends had all held the knife.

"Well, it seems like you no sooner come in contact with someone than they are murdered or knocked senseless." Granddad held out a ticket with her name on it. The destination was Arizona. "It would be safest for you—and probably everyone else—if you were far away. Your great-aunts will keep an eye on you."

"No! Granddad!" Francie pleaded, but she could see he would not relent. "Let me have the box at least," she begged.

"Oh, no," Granddad said. "I think not. That thing is what started all this trouble."

"But—"

"No ifs, ands, or buts," Granddad said. "Here's something to keep you busy while you're in Arizona." Theo handed her a packet of papers. She recognized it. The college applications she hadn't filled out yet. "You should get cracking on that essay," he said.

"I can't go to Arizona! Not now!" What about all the unanswered questions? Who had clonked the museum lady on the head and why? Who had hidden the box in such a weird place? Had someone really murdered Reginald Skitterly? What of the mysterious plant he wanted to find? Was there more to the box than she knew? Someone had to figure all this out. Why shouldn't it be her?

She knew that argument wouldn't win over her grandfather, so instead she said, "What about school? I have tests coming up. And I can't go like this—look at my clothes!" She gestured to her parka and winter boots.

"Your aunts will take you shopping for appropriate clothes," he added, handing her a roll of bills. "Put that away in your wallet now." Granddad pointed to the cash.

"Look at it this way, Sis," Theo said, giving her a sardonic glance in the rearview mirror. "While I'm here, toiling away in boring Minnesota, you get to go somewhere! Have some excitement in your life."

19
ARIZONA

Francie stepped out of the airport in Tucson still swathed in her down jacket and wool stocking hat. First things first, she thought, pulling off her cap and unzipping her jacket. She didn't take her jacket off, though—it wasn't that warm. Jeannette had texted that she and Astrid had gotten tangled up in traffic, so they'd be a little late. Francie decided to do something she knew she should have done long ago: call Nels.

"Hi," Francie said when he answered. "It's me."

"I tried calling you like a million times!" he said. "You never answer your phone."

"My phone is on the bottom of the lake," Francie said. "Like I might have been if Theo hadn't rescued me."

"What?"

"Yeah, I almost died, Nels," Francie said.

"I didn't know."

"No, you didn't know because you didn't make any effort to find out. You just assumed I was avoiding you."

"Okay, fair enough," Nels said. "Were you in the hospital or something?"

"No."

"And you're okay now?"

"Yeah."

"So you maybe could have gotten in touch with me?"

"Yeah," she admitted with a sigh. "But there's been so much—so much going on, my head is swimming."

"Okay," Nels said. "I get it. I'm just one more thing to keep track of."

Was he? Francie wondered. Maybe he was. She didn't say anything.

"You're supposed to object now," he said, "and tell me I'm the most important thing in your life." When she didn't answer, he said, "Or . . . not."

"A lot of stuff going on." Francie felt like crying. She wished he were there right now, with his arms around her or holding her hand in his big, warm paws. She pictured him this past summer—tanned, his sun-bleached hair mussed by the wind. She remembered how he'd emerged from the lake like a kind of Greek god. Neptune, she had thought, if Neptune was young and gorgeous. She remembered him rain-soaked and heroic as he'd rescued her one stormy night on the lake . . .

"Okay, look," Nels said, interrupting her memories. "It's hard. You're there. I'm here. It's your senior year. You should be going to parties and dances and prom and stuff."

Parties and dances and prom? "I'm not. It's life stuff, Nels," Francie said. "I'm trying to find out about my mom."

"Your mom? I thought she was, I thought she . . . I mean, isn't she . . . ?"

"Dead?" Francie finished his sentence. "No. I told you she was dead because that was the story, okay? But she isn't, and now I'm trying to find her, and things have gotten crazy."

"Wow. Sometime I hope you'll tell me everything," Nels said. "But right now you need a break from us—that's what I'm hearing."

Did she? No, she didn't! She wanted it just like it had been last summer. Maybe what she wanted was to have summer back.

A small red Toyota approached, the two passengers inside waving enthusiastically at Francie. The Aunts.

"How about this?" Nels said. "Let's just see how it is when we see each other next summer. See you next summer?"

"Yeah," Francie said, watching the car pulling up in front of her. "That sounds good, Nels. I'll see you next summer."

They hung up as the car came to a stop in front of Francie. *Well, there goes my boyfriend,* Francie thought.

The aunts scrambled out of the car. Jeannette was the taller and thinner of the two, and was wearing flowy slacks and a loose blouse. Astrid, shorter and rounder, wore a flouncy dress with leggings a little baggy at the knees, with her silvery hair done up in a bun on top of her head, wisps of hair floating about like clouds. Both Astrid and Jeannette did some clucking and cooing, then swooped Francie up in their arms, into the car, and away from the airport.

And certainly not directly into the desert. Instead it seemed like everywhere was city, city, city. Lights and traffic, lights and traffic. On and on they drove, past shopping malls and golf courses, past developments tucked behind adobe walls, and more malls and golf courses and hotels, and more housing developments, until finally the lights of the city receded behind them, the road narrowed, and they turned onto a dirt road that twisted and wove through a whole bunch of eerily shaped plants

Francie only caught glimpses of in the headlights. Finally, they pulled up in front of a little, low-slung cottage.

"Here we are at our casita!" Aunt Astrid chirped. The car's tires crunched on the gravel parking spot and came to a stop.

Did she want something to eat or drink? Did she want to talk, to shower, to go to bed? The aunts wanted to know.

Francie just wanted to go to bed, and Astrid showed her to the spare room and gave her a nightgown to wear.

"You seem a little blue, dear," Astrid said.

"I suppose Granddad told you about all the trouble I'm in."

"Well, *he* calls it trouble," Astrid said, turning back the bed covers. "We call it detective work, don't we?"

Francie let out a rueful laugh. Ever since she'd played a detective on a Disney Channel show, her aunts had gotten the idea—and never given it up—that Francie actually was a detective. "I'm not really a detective, Auntie," she said.

"So you say," Astrid said. She busied herself at the window. "Shall we leave the window open a little? It's cool but so pleasant, don't you think?"

Francie nodded.

Aunt Astrid turned from the window and gazed at her for a moment. "Things will get better."

"Maybe," Francie said, "but it doesn't feel that way. I lost something I've looked for all my life. Something I thought would lead me to Mom, but didn't. I feel like instead of *finding* her I just keep *losing* her, over and over. I'm in trouble at school, and Granddad and Theo are both mad at me. Oh, also, I'm probably in trouble with the law. And, well, I guess I just broke up with my boyfriend." She let out a sad laugh. "Maybe I just wrote my college entrance essay on the subject, Who am I? Answer: total loser."

Astrid put her hand on Francie's shoulder. "When you feel like you have lost everything," she said, "that's the moment when you can find yourself." She went out, closing the door behind her.

Francie slipped into the offered nightgown and then into the crisp, cool sheets and under the warm woolen blanket. Outside the window some kind of creature—a bird?—was calling, "Woe." The answer came from a distance, another mournful "Woe."

Woe is right, Francie thought. I should not be here. I should have defied Granddad and stayed at home. But what was it Aunt Astrid had said? Something about when you lose everything, that's when you can find yourself?

What would it mean to find herself? She'd been so busy looking for her mother, she hadn't thought about trying to find her own self. Who was she? That was the question everyone must face at some point or other, especially when it comes time to write a college entrance essay.

The next morning, Francie rose early and watched the mountains turning pink as the sun rose. The color first struck their rocky tops, then crept down the mountainsides as the sun grew higher in the sky. It was beautiful—no doubt about that—but Francie was restless and itchy. All those unsolved mysteries left behind. Had someone been trying to kill Miss Schell? Had *she* hidden the box or had the assailant hidden it? Where had Mr. T. gone? Was he the assailant? Or was he in danger? Was the plant collector really murdered? Most important, now without either Mr. Skitterly or the box, how, how, how was she ever going to find out more about her mother?

As the sunlight reached the base of the mountain and began creeping across the desert, she resolved, *If there was anything to be learned from her aunts, then she wasn't going to waste time: she was going to get right down to finding out what that might be.*

But first there were morning chores: filling bird feeders and making breakfast. The backyard—if you could call it a yard, as there was no grass to be seen—was alive with rabbits, weird little ground squirrels, mourning doves, and some funny quail with curlicues on their heads that wobbled like dashboard bobbleheads when they moved. They were the ones that called "Woe" to each other all night and were still doing it this morning. Cute but sad little birds, Francie thought, while the hummingbirds that thronged the feeder seemed positively giddy about everything—especially the fresh sugar water Astrid had supplied this morning.

Once the chores were done, Francie resolved to ask her aunts what they knew about her mother.

She found Astrid at the kitchen table playing with a coin, and she opened her mouth to ask a question, but Astrid spoke first. "See this coin?" She held it between the thumb and forefinger of her left hand so the coin stood up on its edge.

"Yes," Francie said, "but, Astrid, I wanted to ask—"

"Now I'm going to transfer it to this hand," Astrid said, bringing her right hand to her left and closing her fist around it. "Here it is in my other hand." With a twinkle in her eye, she held up her closed fist.

Jeannette sat down with a cup of coffee and explained. "Astrid is learning magic."

"Proving that you can teach an old aunt new tricks," Astrid said, opening her left hand to reveal that it was empty.

"Okay," Francie said, "but I want to ask something about—"

The coin clattered onto the table, falling from Astrid's other hand. "Oops," she said. "I haven't quite perfected it yet. The trick is to distract. The spectator's eyes will go to the hand that is moving—"

"Cool," Francie interrupted, blurting out, "but I really need to know about Mom. I need to know what you know."

"Well, for one thing," Jeannette said, stopping to take a sip of coffee, "this is where your mother grew up."

"Here," Francie repeated, a little stunned.

"Not in this casita," Jeannette went on. "In the ranch house." She pointed her spoon toward the mountains.

"Ranch . . . ?" Francie repeated.

"Would you like to see it?" Astrid asked. "We'll take you there."

Francie nodded dumbly.

"Yes, she grew up on a ranch," Jeannette said. "Your great-granddaddy owned quite a lot of land. Besides the ranch, this place." She waved her spoon around in a circle indicating the surrounding area. "Your grandfather—I'm talking about your mother's father, of course—when he sold this part, he carved out a parcel for family. This is our little corner, you might say."

"Ever encroached upon," Astrid grumbled.

Francie was aware, beyond the cooing doves and the woe-ing quail, of the distant whine of traffic, an incessantly barking dog at some faraway property, and even farther away, a siren.

Her mother was from here, she thought, staring out at the winter-bare branches of trees and shrubs she didn't know the names of, birds she had never seen before—except, in the case of the roadrunner, as a cartoon character. Mountains of ever-changing colors, and all the otherworldly plants: cacti shaped like barrels, others that looked like piles of crazily stacked salad plates, some with long, snaky arms, and then the big saguaros—

tall, tubular giants with their stubby arms. All of them covered in needles, prickers, spines—as unfriendly as plants could be.

The landscape was strange, foreign, and, it seemed to Francie, a little dangerous with its rattlesnakes, scorpions, and all the other prickers, pokers, and stabbers.

She had never stopped to wonder about how or where her mother had lived in her young life. Come to think of it, she didn't wonder much about anybody else's life. Like Raven, whom she knew to have a different life from her own, with a lot of relatives living on the reservation—her dad, her grandmother, cousins, and probably friends, too. Raven stayed there sometimes. What was that like? Francie had no idea.

Maybe she would understand Raven better if she made an effort to understand how she lived. Once everything settled down, she thought, she would do that. Maybe she'd take Raven up on her offer to make porcupine quill earrings with her grandma. Even if it meant pulling quills out of dead porcupines.

And maybe if Francie understood this place, she would come to better understand her mother, and—who knows?—possibly also herself.

Tomorrow, the aunts said, they'd take a picnic and go visit the ranch. Today they would take Francie shopping for some appropriate clothes and show her around the town. Francie had always wanted a pair of cowboy boots. Maybe she'd use that wad of bills from Granddad to buy herself a pair. Why not?

"Do you want to know how to do the coin trick?" Astrid asked, pulling Francie's mind back to the breakfast table.

"Yes, sure," Francie said. "Why not?"

20
THE RANCH HOUSE

THE CAR HAD STEADILY CLIMBED out of the desert to what was called the high chaparral. Winter grass covered the ground like bright yellow hair, all wind-combed in one direction. In the background lurked charcoal-colored, snow-topped mountains, their grassy foothills peppered with dark piñon trees.

Staring out the window of the back seat, Francie asked her aunts, "Why do you think Mom disappeared?"

"It could have been something to do with her work," Jeannette said, as an old, obviously abandoned ranch appeared. Fences and wooden outbuildings weathered to gray. A broken gate, a sagging roof, a missing door. The rambling, cobbled-together house, all one level—as ranch houses were, Francie reminded herself—looked forlorn in its abandoned state.

"Or, well, we don't like to think about it, but there's another possibility," Astrid said as Jeannette brought the car to a stop.

"What's that?" Francie said.

They piled out of the car, and Astrid spread her arms to indicate the ranch, saying, "It has to do with this."

"The ranch?" Francie asked.

Astrid nodded, adding, "And its demise."

"What happened?" Francie asked. "Why is it abandoned?"

The three of them walked toward a lone picnic table not far from the ranch house. Francie carried the small cooler containing their lunch, while Jeannette and Astrid told the story of a once-prosperous cattle ranch, especially lucky because it had water—a reliable stream that supplied water consistently year-round.

"Back when your great-granddaddy had this place they grazed some thirty thousand head of cattle. The ranch was still doing well when your granddaddy took over. Then something went awry. The water was poisoned."

"Poisoned!" Francie yelped.

"Follow me," Jeannette said, leading Francie to the edge of the bank, where they stood under a couple of blackened cottonwood trees, bare of leaves. She gestured to the orange-stained soil along the stream where neon orange liquid trickled along. "It's been forty years and the water's still contaminated."

"And will be for at least the next 960 years!" Astrid shouted from the picnic table. "That's how long this stuff stays toxic."

"How did that happen?" Francie asked as she and Jeannette walked away from the little creek.

"Upstream from here there was a silver mine," Jeannette explained. "When that mine was no longer profitable, the company just moved on, letting their mining waste contaminate streams and groundwater. The mine waste is full of arsenic, lead, all kinds of toxic metals. Kills everything it touches. Gone are the fish. Gone are the frogs. Cattle didn't fare so well, either."

"Didn't the mine have to clean it up?"

"No. That's the way the law worked back then. Mine doesn't make money—walk away, leave the pollution for someone else to clean up. Billions of dollars and it doesn't end," Jeannette said as they reached the picnic table. "It's happening all over the country. Every day, more than twenty million gallons of untreated, contaminated water streams from these old mine sites. Enough pollution to fill more than two thousand tanker trucks. *Every day*," Jeannette said.

"Jeannette's been studying up on this," Astrid clarified.

"But they can't do that anymore, can they?" Francie asked. "I mean, the companies can't just let all that pollution keep flowing, can they?"

"Nowadays they claim bankruptcy and then walk away, still leaving the expensive mess for someone else to clean up. Someone else being the taxpayers."

"And you think this might have something to do with Mom's disappearance?" Francie wondered.

"We don't like to think so, but when she found out that there are mining interests poised to start sulfide ore mining in the Enchantment Lake watershed, your mother vowed to do what she could to stop them from destroying the pristine waterways and wilderness of our north woods the way they destroyed the ranch and its river."

"We'll finish the story over lunch," Astrid said. "But if you want to peek inside the house, go ahead."

Wandering through the rooms, Francie was overcome with melancholy. Although there were a few furnishings here and there—a rug on the floor, a picture on a wall, an empty vase on a table—most must have been removed. The worn wood floors, the faded, chipped paint on the doors and window frames, the house's emptiness all combined to feed a feeling of abandonment. In some ways, Francie felt like the house looked: a porch that listed slightly, sagging floors, the colors of the walls faded into the desert hues of sand, rock, dust.

She couldn't help wondering, as she roamed from room to room, had her mother eaten in this kitchen? Played on this screen porch? Then she came to what was surely a bedroom, which at this moment was suffused with early afternoon light, its dusty peach–colored walls seeming to almost glow. She could picture the lace curtains at the window. The brass bed covered with a cowboy-themed bedspread. A simple chest of drawers.

Now there was only one thing: a bookcase, with books still on the shelves. Francie ran her finger over their spines. Her mother's books? she wondered. She tilted her head to read the titles. *Black Beauty. The Adventures of Remi. Wind in the Willows. The Big Book of Fairy Tales.* Fairy tales, Francie thought. Wasn't the ditty about the island and the church, wasn't that from a fairy tale? She slipped *The Big Book of Fairy Tales* out of the cupboard. It fell open to a story titled "The Giant Who Had No Heart in His Body." That was the story! It was about a giant who had turned six brothers to stone, and the youngest brother had to rescue the others and destroy the giant. But the giant was not easily destroyed because he never carried his heart with him. He had hidden it away where it could never be found.

Francie sat down on the wide windowsill with the sun on her back and turned to the end of the story where the troll finally reveals where he had hidden his heart: inside an egg that was inside a duck that was swimming in a well that was inside a church that was on an island in a lake. *That* was what was inside the egg . . . the giant's heart!

Her eye snagged on a couple of loose pieces of paper that were stuck into the pages of the book. One looked like a page torn from a different book—different typeface, different kind of paper. It read:

Far away and long ago there was a land where all the people had remarkable memories. In fact, they never forgot a single thing. People traveled from all around to eat of a plant that was said to restore memory. But one day, an evil giant put a spell over the land, causing snow to fall relentlessly and everything to sleep for thousands of years.

Francie turned the paper over, assuming the story went on, but the other side was blank. The other piece of paper was an article torn from a newspaper. It told about paleontologists who had discovered ancient bones and fossils that had been exposed on an eroded riverbank in Siberia. More than 120 feet below the permafrost, among these bones, squirrels had made burrows where they had cached seeds—hundreds of thousands of seeds from a variety of plant species. Some of the seeds had been recovered, but others had mysteriously disappeared before botanists had an opportunity to study them. This was especially disappointing, the article stated, "since it was thought that some of the seeds may have come from a long extinct and storied plant."

More stories of seeds from extinct plants! And now a story about a plant that could restore memory. Was it possible that the box had once contained seeds from a plant that could somehow restore memory? That would explain why the box was considered so valuable. And why a lot of people would want to possess it. But now the box was empty ... wasn't it?

Francie reinserted the loose pages, closed the book, tucked it under her arm, and went outside to show all this to the aunts.

"You seem very thoughtful, dear," Astrid said, as Francie sat down at the picnic table.

"I found something," Francie said, setting the book on the table and opening it to the loose pages.

The aunts studied the pages while Francie munched on a chicken sandwich and contemplated the significance of the papers and the fact that they were placed with the story she remembered from her childhood. She remembered Mr. T. saying that her mother left clues when she'd been younger. Had her mother left these clues for her? But how could her mother ever have known that she would come to Arizona—to this ranch—and pull that book off the shelf?

Or was her mother much closer and much more aware of what was going on than she thought? She swept her eye over the scene wondering, *Just where was Iris Frye?*

In any case, Francie did not see how mining tied into any of this. Maybe it didn't. Yet the aunts thought it might, and in her experience her aunts' hunches were often right.

She had just taken a bite out of a devilishly spicy deviled egg—sprinkled accidentally with cayenne instead of paprika—when her phone rang.

"It's Theo," she told her aunts and picked up.

"Listen to me," Theo said, before she could even utter a word of greeting.

Something was wrong. Francie sat very still and listened as he went on. "There are some guys here—"

"Guys?" Francie said. "What guys?"

Her aunts looked up from their sandwiches and Francie glanced at them.

"They haven't exactly given their names," Theo said, "but, uh, they seem anxious to talk to Mom."

Voices in the background said something and Theo corrected himself. "That is, talk to her face to face."

"Well, so do I, but since nobody knows where she is—"

"It's important," Theo said.

"Sweetheart," a new voice—a man's—addressed Francie over the phone. "You get message to your mother." He said "mother" like "*maawder*," with some kind of strange accent. "We need to speak to her, pronto. We got this box here. Your *braawder*—nice guy—he's here, too. But, the thing is, see, we need to see your *maawma*. Soon. Hard to say what happens otherwise. Thirty-six hours, okay?"

"I have no idea where—" Francie said.

"Next instruction will come at school office. Not for you, for your mother only. In meantime, tell no one. No police. Nobody. Anything like that, we disappear and so does box. Your brother . . . good guy, your brother. It would be shame if something happened to him. You know what I'm saying?"

Theo came on the line again. "I'm sorry, Sis," he said. "But I have confidence in you. *You can do it.*"

The line went dead.

Francie looked at her aunts. They looked at her. They looked stricken. Francie felt stricken. "Do you have any idea where Mom is?" Francie begged.

They shook their heads and in unison whispered, "What are we going to do?"

Wind rattled the tall, dry weeds, and down by the stream the bare branches of the cottonwoods waved, casting crooked black shadows on the yellow grass below. Francie stared past the aunts at the two gnarled trees, standing like ancient spinster sisters guarding the dry creek bed, sisters having grown nearly identical in their old age: you wouldn't have been able to tell one from the other.

You can do it, Theo had said.

Maybe she could, Francie thought. Maybe she just could.

21
A VERY IMPORTANT ROLE

IN ORDER TO PLAY the most important role of her life, Francie was going to need some help. She had thought it through on the long sleepless night of flights and airport layovers.

Now she stood hopping from one frozen foot to the other behind the mobile classrooms, which were really just double-wide trailers—cold in the winter, hot in the summer—waiting for Raven to walk by on her way to school.

"Hey," she said, catching her friend by the arm.

"You're home!" Raven said when she realized who was under the parka hood and scarf.

"No, I really am not."

"So you're a figment of my imagination?"

"I need you to help me be my mother."

"I'm sorry," Raven said. "It sounded like you said that you needed me to help you be your mother."

"Yes, that's what I said."

"Did you get too much sun down there in the desert? Suffering from heatstroke?"

"I need to pretend to be my mom, and I'm going to need help."

"You are doing some crazy, dangerous thing, aren't you?" Raven crossed her arms, signaling her displeasure. "And you're going to get into trouble—again. And I am not going to help you do that!"

"Listen to me," Francie said. "It's for Theo. He's the one who's in trouble."

"What?" Raven grabbed Francie's arms. "How?"

"Someone nabbed him," Francie said. "Kidnapped! The only way to get him back is if Mom shows up. Nobody knows where she is or *if* she is, so I'm going to be her. The clock is ticking away!"

"Oh my God, Francie!" Raven said. "But call the police! That's what you should do. Don't go get yourself kidnapped, too!"

"No police. Sorry, but it just can't be. I'll explain it all later. It's really urgent. We have to hurry. This has to happen today!"

"You're really serious!"

"Yes, I'm serious. And I need your help. I need makeup and something to wear. Not this." Francie gestured at her jeans, clompy winter boots, and parka. "How do we get into the costume shop?"

"Jay has a key. He's doing tech for the play, so Ms. Hanover gave him one."

"Let's meet at the costume shop at lunch. Totally secret."

Raven nodded and sprinted away.

Francie sprinted away, too, right into the farthest-tucked-away booth at Vi's Café. Realizing she hadn't eaten since the deviled eggs the day before, she ordered French toast and bacon, hot chocolate, and orange juice. Since she hadn't slept much either, she also ordered coffee.

"Honey," Vi said, looking at Francie over her glasses, "why aren't you at school?"

"Independent study," Francie said, setting her laptop on the table in front of her.

Vi raised one pencil-thin eyebrow but didn't say anything—just sauntered away with a shake of her head.

Francie flipped open her laptop and typed in "sulfide ore copper mining."

Her hot chocolate went cold as she read about the worst environmental catastrophe in Canada: a dam collapsed releasing twenty-five million cubic meters of copper and gold mining tailings and wastewater into a pristine glacial lake, filling it instead with thick, gray sludge. In Brazil there was a similar dam collapse; this time, in addition to environmental damage, 270 people were killed.

She ignored her breakfast when it was set on the table, instead riveted to an article that explained that the proposed dam in their area was the same design as the two she'd just been reading about. The company names associated with the proposed Minnesota mines were ConiMet and Glentech. *Glentech*, she thought. She pulled out the card from the unfortunately named Louis Streife. Yep, Glentech. So he was involved in mining?

"Your breakfast is getting cold, girl," Vi said. "What are you studying?"

"Copper-nickel mining," Francie said.

"That would bring jobs. It'd be real good for our economy," Vi said.

Francie looked up. "Would it? It seems like it's environmentally disastrous. It's really ruined other places. And what about the tourist economy? It seems like that's what keeps this place really going. What happens if the water is ruined?"

Vi poured more coffee into Francie's mostly full cup.

"Well, honey," Vi said. "That laptop you're using? That smarty-pants phone you got?" She pointed at Francie's phone, lying on the table. "Gotta have copper to make those things. Where do you think it's going to come from?"

The café door jingled, and Vi turned her head. "Gotta go," she said, trotting off.

"Is it worth it?" Francie mumbled.

After reading more, and only poking at her breakfast, she glanced at the time and saw she better hustle to meet Raven and Jay at the costume shop. Her research hadn't gotten her any closer to knowing more about who might have kidnapped her brother or why, nor did she have any more clues about where her mother might be.

But now it was time to put her plan in place.

Francie, still consumed and disguised by her parka hood and scarf, converged on the costume shop at the same time as Raven and Phoebe. Jay swung the door open and waved the three girls inside. While Phoebe swept in, Francie pulled Raven aside and whispered, "Why is she here?"

"Makeup," Raven said. "She's the best."

"What about the gossip problem?"

"No, she's cool. She's stoked to help out."

Francie sincerely hoped so, as she and Raven followed Phoebe inside.

The costume shop was basically a large closet stuffed full of donated prom and bridesmaid dresses, ratty mink coats, a penguin costume, a lion's mane, something unidentifiable constructed out of aluminum foil, and other random donations.

Francie sat down at the makeup counter and, while Phoebe studied her in the mirror, Francie turned to Jay.

"Got your tablet?" she asked.

"Of course he does!" Raven shouted from somewhere in the racks of clothes.

"See what you can find out about these companies." Francie handed Jay a piece of paper upon which she'd written "ConiMet" and "Glentech."

"Well, Glentech is a pharmaceutical company," Jay said. "We've got Glentech notepads and coffee mugs and stuff like that all over our house. My dad's a dentist," he explained to Phoebe.

So what did a pharmaceutical company have to do with mining? Francie wondered.

"So you want to look how old?" Phoebe asked Francie's reflection.

"Mid-to-late forties," Francie answered.

"No problem," Phoebe said as she started selecting bottles and jars and brushes and wands out of the bins of makeup on the counter. "It helps that you already look so much older than you are," she said, then quickly added, "I mean that in a good way."

Raven emerged from the back of the room carrying a pencil skirt and fitted jacket. Also a pair of black boots with spike heels.

"I can't wear those!" Francie cried. "Or that tight skirt. What if I have to run?"

"Run?" Phoebe's interest was piqued. "Are you on a case? Is this for some kind of detective thing? Oh my gawd! Is it about what happened to the lady at the museum?"

"Yeah, Phoebe," Francie said. "And we're trusting you to keep it totally, totally secret. If you tell anyone—anyone!—it could blow our whole undercover investigation."

"I mean, I am silent!" Phoebe mimed zipping her lips shut. "Nothing from me. OMG! I've got goosebumps!" She held out her arm for Francie to inspect. "First, let's put your hair up." She deftly brushed, then twisted, then pinned Francie's hair into something she called a "chignon."

"Whoa," Jay said softly.

"What?" Francie asked.

"Look at this." Jay held out his tablet. "Those dark squares you see just about everywhere? That's all mineral exploration—copper-nickel. Apparently there's a lot of it under our feet."

Francie stared at the map, feeling slightly nauseous. The colored squares seemed to consume everything that wasn't water.

"Ahem?" Phoebe said, waving a mascara wand at Francie.

Francie turned back to the mirror, and Phoebe applied false eyelashes, mascara, eyeliner, and Francie didn't know what all to her face.

Next, Phoebe pointed an eyebrow pencil at Francie. "Scrunch up your face like this." Phoebe squeezed together the features of her face, knitting her eyebrows and pulling her lips together in a tight little knot.

Francie copied her, asking, "Why am I doing this?"

"So I can see where the wrinkles are going to be when you get them. LOL. I mean *if* you get them." Phoebe began tracing the creases in Francie's face with the dark pencil.

"Not too much!" Francie held up a hand. "It's not stage makeup!"

Phoebe held out several tubes of lipstick. "What color, do you think?" she tilted her head sideways, studying Francie's face.

"Just a minute," Francie said and dug in her pocket, retrieving the lipstick she'd found on the floor of her bathroom—*aubergine* the color was called. "Try this," she said.

"Ooh," Phoebe said, applying it. "Nice effect!"

Francie took a quick glance in the mirror to see her face transformed: her eyes lined and lashes darkened, eyebrows arched, lips full and aubergined, and hair done in a kind of austere bun on the back of her head. Was this her mother's face? Is this what her mother looked like now? Was this the color of her mother's lipstick? In fact, was this her mother's lipstick? Had her mother left it in Francie's apartment? And yet she had not bothered to get in touch with Francie. If she was here, why didn't she contact her daughter or son? Was this all a big game to her? A big game of hide-and-seek with her own children?

A flush rose to Francie's cheeks. She thought perhaps the top of her head might blow off, she was so angry.

"Wow," Phoebe said softly. "You look . . . dangerous."

And older, Francie thought, observing herself in the mirror. The tight lips and set jaw, the arched eyebrows. She would have to remember that. Anger made her look older.

"Here's something," Jay said. "This big multinational corporation Flocore owns more than 70 percent of ConiMet's stock."

"What does that mean?"

"It means Flocore is the majority shareholder of the mining company. It means that Flocore, not ConiMet, owns the mine and all its profits. And Flocore is being investigated for," Jay read from his screen, "money laundering, making corrupt mining and oil deals across the globe, bribery, displacing indigenous people, and environmental and human rights violations worldwide.' The corporation and its chief executives have been linked to a lot of nasty stuff—like to a paramilitary group in South America responsible for murdering trade unionists."

These people are capable of some serious misdeeds, Francie thought. Might they have threatened her mother in some way? To keep her from her investigating?

"Look what I found!" Raven called, emerging from the far reaches of the room, carrying what looked like a dead animal. It turned out to be a coat with a wide collar of thick fur and a Russian-style hat made of the same champagne-colored fur.

"Huh!" Phoebe said. "I've never seen that before! What kind of fur is it?"

"I think it's fox," Raven said. "You've got to wear it, Frenchy. It would look so fabulous on you—and the way you look—"

She set the fox fur hat on Francie's head and let out a kind of half-sigh, half-gasp. "Sha-zam! You're . . . gorgeous!" she said.

"You look . . . like Angelina Jolie," Jay said.

"Not *that* old!" Phoebe said.

"You have to wear the hat," they all said together.

"And the coat," Raven said, holding it out in such a way that Francie found herself sliding her arms into the sleeves.

"And the boots," Phoebe said, holding out the stiletto-heeled boots. "They're going to make you look sooo sophisticated."

"Not if I can't walk in them!"

"Try them," Raven coaxed.

Francie ducked behind the racks of costumes, put everything on, even the boots, then stepped out.

At first, silence.

"OMG." That was Phoebe.

"Wow," Raven whispered.

"Hot!" Jay squeaked.

Phoebe and Raven gave him the side-eye and cracked up.

"Hey, one other thing?" Jay said. "Both those companies, Glentech and ConiMet? They're both subsidiaries of that same corrupt multinational corporation."

"What does that mean?" Francie asked.

Jay shrugged. "I don't know. Just thought it was an interesting detail."

Francie paused for a moment to consider that, then stood, teetering a little on the heels. "Now I have to go to the office," she said.

Jay, Raven, and Phoebe stared back at her slack-jawed.

"You're going to the *school* office?" Phoebe asked. "Why?"

"I have to stop there—can't explain," Francie said.

"But Candee and Pat," Phoebe said, "they *know* you."

Exactly, Francie thought. She had figured out that was the whole reason why the kidnappers had chosen to leave a message there. If the secretaries had been told the message was to be delivered to Francie's mother and not to Francie, they would deliver only to the mother. The secretaries were real sticklers that way: maybe that's how the kidnappers could be sure the message went to the right person.

"Well, this will be the test," she said. "And I'm a trained actor, right?" She squared her shoulders, pulled herself to her full height, and lengthened her neck. Her mother would be elegant, sophisticated, graceful—a lot of things Francie wasn't. But she was an actor, so she could pretend to be those things. "And if I can convince the secretaries in the main office, I can convince anyone . . . right?"

Francie's friends nodded slowly.

"But if anyone asks, you haven't seen me. Okay?"

They nodded again.

"Okay. I'm going out the back way and coming around through the front doors."

"Can we watch?" Jay asked.

Raven and Phoebe sitting on each side of him punched him on each arm.

"No, you idiot!" Raven said.

Phoebe looked at her phone. "We're supposed to be at lunch right now. We better get in there so our absence doesn't arouse suspicion."

Jay and Raven turned to stare at her.

"What?" she said. "Am I right?"

Francie smiled at Phoebe. "You're exactly right. Thanks, Phoebe. And you guys." She took off the hat and smoothed her hair.

"Wear the hat, French," Phoebe said, touching her arm as she went out. "And good luck."

. . . . .

Who is Iris? Who is Iris? Who is Iris? Francie wondered as she tried to find a graceful stride in the heeled boots. Just before she pulled open the door to the main office, she took a deep breath and told herself, *I am Iris.* Then she plunged into the office and immediately caught the attention of everyone inside: the two secretaries and a couple of eighth grade boys, who were loitering by the counter with their mouths hanging open. She touched them on their chins and said in a husky voice several notches lower than her own, "Catching flies?"

She turned to the secretaries who were staring like the eighth graders. Lowering her voice another few notches, she said, "My daughter Francesca Frye is a student here, I believe."

"Oh, Francie?" squeaked Candee. "Yes, she is. But she hasn't been in school for several days."

"Yes, I'm aware," Francie said and made a show of looking at the nameplates on their desks. She already knew that the two of them were not at their right desks, so she added, "Pat."

"Oh, I'm not Pat. I'm Candee. That's Pat," Candee said, pointing to Pat.

"My mistake," Francie glanced at Pat whose initial stunned look had morphed into something else. Skepticism?

"Wow," Pat said. "You and Francie are the spitting image of each other."

"So people say," Francie said.

"We knew you were around," Candee said.

"Oh?" Francie said. "How?"

"Well, you signed Francie's permission slip for the field trip!" Candee said, holding up a form. "We were surprised—I mean we were delighted, of course, because we thought . . . well, I mean . . . I guess . . ."

Francie shut her down with a menacing glower.

Candee giggled nervously, and Pat shot her a glance as if to say, *Not appropriate.*

Meanwhile, Francie really wondered what she had done. She had brought her mother to life by simply forging her signature—and now by impersonating her. What if her mother really was dead? What kind of a strange surreal mess might she have created? Could it be any worse than the current mess?

"Oh!" Candee exclaimed. "There's a message for you!"

Pat squinted at Francie and said softly, "I'd almost, almost say you *were* Francie."

Francie needed to get out of there before Pat recognized what was going on.

Candee giggled uncomfortably. "But Francie would know our names, Pat."

"And, well, there are certain age differences," Pat added.

"Ho ho, that too!" Candee chortled.

"Well, then, the message?" Francie said, holding out her gloved hand into which Candee placed the sealed envelope. "Thank you very much." She pivoted and swished out of the office toward the main doors of the school. *Nobody follow me. Nobody follow me,* she thought, sweating bullets under the warm coat and fur hat. As soon as she left the school, she opened the coat to the wind and let the frigid air shock her back to her senses.

You better buck up, her senses told her. *You've got a tougher and more dangerous audience ahead.*

22
BIRCH GROVE

FRANCIE RIPPED OPEN THE ENVELOPE and unfolded the single sheet of paper on which was a single line: *Further instructions at Birch Grove. Inquire at nurses' station.*

Birch Grove, the nursing home? Where Loretta lived? Strange place to leave a message, but whatever. Francie headed straight there.

A small cluster of residents sat hunched in wheelchairs as Francie entered the lobby. Some of them twisted around to look at her; some didn't seem to notice. A couple of nurse's aides who'd been chatting at the front desk looked up as she came toward them, wearing *We are not going to let on how surprised we are* expressions. All heads at the nurses' station moved in unison, following Francie with their gaze until she stopped in front of them.

She knew she'd have to pretend she'd never been here before if she wanted the whole ruse to work.

"I'm Iris Frye," she said, cursing the overly bright lights that flooded the lobby. "There should be a message for me?"

"A message?" one of the aides said, making a show of looking on her desk for a message.

Francie nodded. The less said the better.

"It must be at the nurses' station at the other side of the building," the aide said. "It's just down that hall, take a right turn, then a left, by the other doors."

On the way to the other nurses' station, Francie passed by Loretta's room.

"My dear!" Loretta called to her through the open door.

Francie stuck her head into the room.

"My, my," Loretta said. "It's been so long! Come in."

Francie stepped into the room and said, "I'm sorry I can't stay and chat. I . . . I have an appointment."

"Well, at least have a jelly bean," Loretta offered, holding the bowl out for her. "Take some for later." She winked. "Because you never know when you might need one."

"Right," Francie snagged several green jelly beans from the bowl and put them in her coat pocket. "See you soon, I hope," Francie said, stepping back into the hall.

A nurse's aide was waiting outside the door for her. Francie recognized her. "Marcie," her name badge read.

"If you're Iris Frye, I have a message for you," Marcie said. Her face stayed neutral, but her mouth was a tight line as she handed Francie an envelope, then pivoted and disappeared down the hallway.

Francie tore open the envelope and read the message: *Go to the public boat landing on Enchantment and wait. Someone will come for you. Come alone. If there is evidence of any law enforcement involvement, or if you are accompanied by anyone, you will not see the item in question again.*

When she looked up, she noticed someone moving toward her in a wheelchair—someone with an astoundingly familiar shock of white hair on his head and his arm in a sling. *Please do not let that be . . . . It can't be . . . . Please, that cannot be Granddad.*

She tamped down the urge to bolt and run, instead walking backwards, hoping she could get to the exit before he reached her. But his electric wheelchair—Why was he in a wheelchair? Why was he even here?—was coming at her at warp speed. She doubted she could outrun it.

She watched as his face transformed from bewilderment to menacing glower. She was supposed to be in Arizona. She was not supposed to be here, acting like her own mother. And if she had returned to Walpurgis, she should be in school right now.

"What the devil?" he said in a hoarse whisper when he got close enough. "Why are you dressed up like a dance-hall floozy?"

Francie glanced at her reflection in a hallway mirror. She wasn't sure what a "floozy" was, but it sounded about right. "What are *you* doing here?" she said.

"I asked you first," he said.

"No, you didn't," Francie said. "You said I looked like some kind of floozy—"

"Well, you know what I meant. I meant, what are you doing here?"

"You explain what you're doing here first."

Their whispered exchange had drawn attention. At the end of the hall an aide started walking swiftly toward them.

"Would you be so kind as to wheel me to my room, Miss?" Granddad said to Francie, transforming his voice to a simpering whine. Then, more tartly, as the nurse's aide came within earshot, "I can never get the staff around here to do anything for me."

Francie crammed the note in her pocket, grabbed the wheelchair handles, and pushed him down the hall.

Once inside Granddad's room, with the door shut, they had

a mutual scolding session that ended when Granddad said, "You're going to blow my cover!"

"Your cover?" Francie said.

"Yes," he answered. "I'm working undercover."

"Here? In a nursing home?"

"Nefarious activities can occur anywhere," he said. "Please get out of that getup and go home."

"Not until you explain about these nefarious activities," Francie said.

He stuck his head out of the door, looked both ways, and popped back into the room, surprisingly spry for a man who had moments before been in a wheelchair.

"Your friend Loretta is being surveilled."

"How do you know that?"

"I think I know surveillance when I see it!" Granddad said, a bit huffily.

"What? How? Never mind!" Francie cried. "This is crazytown. I have to go. I cannot talk to you."

"Cannot talk to me!" Granddad said in a huff.

Francie hastily filled him in on what had happened to Theo, and the call she'd had. She told him that no one could know about any of this—probably not even (or especially not) Granddad. So he had to keep it to himself. And, no, she was *not* going to tell him where she was going.

"This is a fine kettle of fish!" he grumbled. "We have to call the FBI!"

"No, no police."

"The FBI is not the police, it's the Federal Bureau of Investigation."

"Let's not split hairs!" Francie scolded, pulling her gloves out of her pockets. "I don't have much time! And you cannot—*cannot*—interfere! Do you understand me?" She put her gloves on, shook a finger at him as if he were a dog, and said, "You stay here."

23

THE RED FISH HOUSE

Francie stood at the boat landing and stared through her false eyelashes, which were growing heavy with frost, out at the frozen lake. A haphazard village of tiny houses, many no bigger than outdoor privies, dotted the lake near the far shore. Ice-fishing houses. Most of them seemed abandoned on a weekday afternoon. Between her and the houses lay a patchwork of white snow and, where the wind had scoured it away, gray or black ice.

The ice, or maybe the water under the ice, moaned like a whale with a bass voice. Or a giant, Francie thought, asleep beneath a coverlet of ice and snow, rolling over with a groan.

A high buzzing whine made her turn to see a snowmobile coming toward her, following along the shore. The snowmobile stopped in front of her, and the snowmobiler took off his helmet. This did nothing to help identify him since he was wearing a balaclava under the helmet. He looked all around, probably to make sure she was alone, and finally asked, "Iris Frye?"

When Francie nodded, he handed her a helmet and gestured for her to climb on behind him.

"Where are we going?" she asked, not putting the helmet on.

The rider turned and pointed at the fish houses. "The red one there," he said.

"You've got to be kidding me," Francie said. "A fish house?"

"Very private," the man said.

Francie did not, under any circumstance, want to go out on ice of any kind. She wondered if this was a test. If they knew anything about her, they probably were aware that she'd fallen through the ice recently. If she hesitated now, would they know she was not the real Iris?

She had to pretend to be a person who was not afraid. Like her mother, who was no doubt fearless, brave, and X-Woman strong. Well, she *was* her mother, she reminded herself, as she put on the helmet and climbed onto the snowmobile behind the driver, pretending with all her might.

In spite of her fear, she had enough wherewithal to notice that the driver did not seem to be going toward the fish houses. Instead, he seemed headed away from them, skirting close to the shore.

She pointed across the lake and shouted, "Why not go that way?"

"Not safe!" he shouted back.

Okay, Francie thought. *Then fine, take the safe way.* She squeezed her eyes shut and wrapped her arms around herself, because for sure she wasn't going to wrap them around Theo's kidnapper.

He parked the snowmobile by a rusty-colored fish house, somewhat set apart from the others. Two other snowmobiles were parked just outside the small building, each with a sled filled with five-gallon buckets, canvas tarps, and a menacing jumble of wicked-looking fishing paraphernalia, including knives, hooks, and ice picks.

The snowmobile driver stayed seated on his machine and pointed at the red fish house. "You're supposed to go there," he said.

Francie extracted herself from the machine, handed the man her helmet, and staggered across the ice, cursing the tight skirt and high-heeled boots and the friend who'd made her wear them. She should have stuck with her clompy winter boots. If she'd known this was where she was going to end up, she would have.

Several dead fish scattered on the ice outside the door did nothing to raise her spirits. Francie flung open the door, and hoping she had not left most of her makeup on the inside of her helmet, stepped inside.

After the vast brightness of the ice-and-snow-covered lake, it took several moments for her eyes to adjust to the windowless darkness inside. The only light came from one large squarish hole in the ice, glowing a watery green.

"Couldn't get a room at the Ritz?" she said to the dark shapes of what she took to be human beings. Three of them. One standing, holding some kind of long pole. One sitting, holding something similar, and one tied to a chair and gagged. That was Theo. She clenched her teeth, holding in the sob that wanted to escape.

The long poles, she realized now, were spears.

Spears, she wondered? Then the one seated on the over-turned five-gallon bucket, intently peering into the hole in the ice, poised his spear over the mesmerizingly bright water, and Francie remembered the dead fish outside the door. Apparently these guys weren't here pretending to fish but were actually fishing—with spears.

As her eyes adjusted, she peered at the one who stood guard

over Theo. The tattoos that snaked around his face and neck made him look like he'd been run over by several fat-tire bikes.

The chair in which Theo was seated teetered perilously close to the hole in the ice. No doubt by design.

Theo's eyes were wide with surprise, confusion, then, when they met Francie's, recognition. He knew who was behind the disguise. Thank goodness he had a gag in his mouth, Francie thought. He should wear one more often.

"I see you managed to snag the troublemaker of my children," Francie said. "Always getting himself into trouble, even as a tot." Theo's eyebrows knit and unknit but he refrained from comment, thanks to the gag. "What has he done and how can I help?" Francie continued.

The guy who'd been seated got up, reached into a duffel bag, and extracted the silver box. Francie's eyes went to it and stayed on it as the man pushed the overturned bucket toward her and set the box on it. Then he looked right at her, and Francie noticed a scar running down one cheek, eerily catching the greenish light from the water-filled hole in the ice.

"Open." He pointed to the box. The flickering light made the scar seem to slither, snakelike, up his face.

Francie licked her lips, tasting her lipstick. Or was it her mother's lipstick? And if it were her mother's, why wasn't her mother here, saving her son? With great deliberation, she took off her gloves, pulling gently on the tip of each finger.

"You open now," said the scarred man, the one with the Russian accent. Francie dubbed him Boris. "I am impatient man."

Francie picked up the box and cradled it as if it were a baby. She reminded herself that she wanted to get what information she could from these thugs, since they must know something about her mother. She turned the box in her hands as if seeing it for the first time, while asking a few questions.

"How did you know I was around here?" she asked.

"We have friends," he said.

Friends? Like school secretaries, she wondered, remembering how Candee had said, "We knew you must be in town."

"And both your kids were around here," he added, "and you like to keep an eye on them, no?"

Was he saying that her mother was nearby, watching them? Then why wasn't she here now? The only way Francie was going to forgive her, Francie decided, was if Iris were dead.

Francie ducked her head and began to retrace the steps to open the box. "So you guys just have nothing better to do than trail me around?" she asked.

"Haha," Boris said, not really laughing. "We go where we're told. Boss says go to godforsaken place in middle of nowhere, we go to godforsaken place in middle of nowhere." He gestured around him, then held up his spear. "Making best of situation."

Her fingers moved along the box. *The lake . . .* then *. . . the island on the lake . . . .* The panel opened, the key appeared. *The church on the island . . . .* The keyhole appeared. She inserted the key; the box opened.

"There you go," she said, holding the box so he could see its emptiness. "It's empty."

Boris set his spear aside and peered inside. "Looks can be deceiving," he said pointedly. "You should know."

Slightly rattled by that statement, she looked at him. What was he saying?

"You should know how to open *all the way*," Boris said, drawing out his filet knife. "Unless you are needing what is in the box to improve your memory."

So, Francie thought, *it must be true what she had deduced about the box's contents. And there must be more to the box than she knew.*

"Give a lady some room to work," she said.

The thugs backed up. Boris began to pick his teeth with the sharp end of the knife.

Francie really had no idea what to do next. She glanced at the hole in the ice, at the water moving about below. *In the church is a well.* What had Raven said about a well? That it represented "depths unknown"? Perhaps as far as the box was concerned there were still depths unknown.

She hoped there were also depths to discover in her memory. She remembered the jelly beans in her pocket. Would that help? She fished one out and popped it into her mouth, tasting the green of a long-ago summer and willing herself back and back, years and years, until she was just a tiny girl with tiny fingers, the box in her hand. And if she could just spring the last panel, just get the box all the way open, figure out the puzzle, her mother would return to her.

As she felt along the bottom, a faded memory came to life, made suddenly sharper by cold, by fear, maybe by necessity. She inched her fingers along the edges for the tiniest of levers, something nearly invisible, something a four-year-old's fingers could have grasped. Then, there—a thread, thin as a hair and light as a whisper.

"Can't you hurry it up?" Boris grunted. He took off his stocking hat and rubbed furiously at his skull.

"You can't rush this process," Francie said. With a gentle tug the bottom gave slightly, tilting under her fingers. She knew there would be something there, something that had been missed before. When she found it, what then? There was no guarantee that if she handed over the prize that these thugs would let Theo go—or her, for that matter. Why would they? After all, there was a very convenient hole in the ice—a handy disposal method for two inconvenient witnesses.

The thought made her begin to tremble, and she had to remind herself that she was no longer Francie. Now she was Iris, who was not afraid.

Her fingers found the object concealed below the false bottom. She didn't dare look but could tell that it was envelope-thin, a size only big enough to hold a few pearls, say, or a necklace of small diamonds, or perhaps even more valuable—a tiny fistful of exceedingly rare, miracle-working seeds.

24
KILLING OF TIME

BORIS LET OUT AN EXASPERATED HUFF. "You just playing," he said, throwing up his arms. "Killing of time!"

Pinching the small packet between her fingers, she held it out for Boris to see.

He was silent, staring at the vacuum-sealed, metallic-looking packet in her fingers, which he was just now realizing was being held over the hole in the ice.

"Hey, hey, hey!" Boris said, eyeing her as if she were a wild animal that had wandered into the fish house.

"Pretty sure this is what you are hoping to find," she said.

When he reached toward her, she pulled her hand back. "Just a few questions first. Are you two responsible for what happened to Skitterly?"

"Who?"

"The plant collector."

The two men looked at each other, then shook their heads. "We don't know him. Hand it over." Boris nodded at the copper-colored packet in Francie's hand and snapped his fingers.

"What about Miss Schell?" she asked.

"Michelle?"

"Miss Schell," Francie said.

"Don't know her either. No more questions. You put the packet in the box—just loose. Then close the box. Then hand the box over to me."

"Why do you need the box?" Francie asked, clutching it tightly.

"Boss wants it," Boris said. "And hurry it up."

Francie felt like she'd rather tear off her own arm before she gave up the box again, but she didn't see how to get around it. Still, she knew the seeds were the important thing, and about those she had an idea.

"Okay, look," Francie said. "I'm going to put this packet back into the box." She held it up so they could clearly see it. "Just loose like this, so it's easy to retrieve." She made a show of putting the seed packet into the box, then shook the box a little so they could hear the slight rattle inside.

"Now I'm closing the box." She closed the lid, put the key back inside the panel, and closed it, then shook it again, to illustrate that the seeds were still inside. "I'll hand it over just as soon as you untie—" She almost said, "my brother" but caught herself, ending with "Theo."

Boris nodded at Tire Tread, who started to untie Francie's brother. Soon, Francie thought, this will all be over, and I can go somewhere and warm up. Her feet were so frozen she couldn't feel them anymore.

Her thoughts were interrupted when the door flew open and Balaclava Man stuck his head in, barked "Cops!" and then backed out, letting the door slam behind him.

The sounds of one departing snowmobile and several approaching ATVs could be clearly heard through the thin walls of the fish house. Boris and Tire Tread both lunged at Francie.

"I didn't call them!" Francie protested as Tire Tread tried to wrench the box away. At the same time, out of the corner of her eye, she saw the flash of the filet knife as Boris moved toward Theo.

"Okay!" Francie shouted as she let go of the box.

Tire Tread stumbled backward and then, to avoid stepping into the hole, lurched forward. Francie gave him a little shove that caught him off guard. The box flew from his hands and splashed into the water where it quickly began to sink.

Now both Boris and Tire Tread were on their knees, scrambling to retrieve the box, yelling things like "Get the net!" and "No, the *net*, stupid!"

Francie pushed past them, reaching Theo just as he freed himself from the loosened ropes. Then brother and sister launched themselves out the door of the red fish house and into the cold.

25

A LITTLE INTERLUDE

CURLED UP AT HER AUNTS' CABIN, wrapped in a down comforter, Francie thanked the sheriff for the rescue. After she and Theo had dashed out of the fish house, they had run toward the approaching ATVs while Boris and Tire Tread leapt on their snow machines and roared away in the opposite direction.

"You have your grandfather to thank for us showing up right then," Sheriff Warner said. "He gave us a call after you left the nursing home."

"Mmm," Francie said, realizing that the kidnappers' note explaining where she should go must have fallen from her pocket when she was in Granddad's room.

"So maybe you'd like to explain what exactly is going on," the sheriff said. "Your grandfather said it pertains to a box."

Francie glanced at Theo, who was leaning against the kitchen doorway behind the sheriff.

"The kidnappers were interested in a box," she acknowledged.

"And what is special about this box?" the sheriff asked.

Francie took a deep breath and said, "They believed that it contained some seeds from an extinct plant."

The sheriff's eyebrows went up. She scribbled in her notebook. "Okay . . . and where is this box now?"

"Either in the lake, lost in the struggle," Francie said. "Or maybe those guys managed to fish it out and they have it."

"And this is the box you retrieved from the museum."

Francie bit her lip, wondering how the sheriff knew about that.

"Yes, I know about that," Sheriff Warner said. "And if it isn't outright theft, it is considered tampering with a crime scene."

"I didn't steal it!" Francie protested. "It was mine!"

Sheriff Warner took off her glasses and rubbed her eyes, then her temples. "Why do I get the feeling there's a lot more you could tell me?"

Francie shrugged. "I don't know. Maybe there's something I'm not thinking of right now. I'm still a little shook up."

"You really endangered yourself with this little escapade," the sheriff said. "You don't have to do everything by yourself, you know. That's what we're here for. If you would have contacted us earlier, we might have been able to catch those two. They're probably in Canada by now. With the snow . . ." Through the window, Francie could see that snow had begun to fall in fat, wet flakes. "But," the sheriff finished, "I have to give you credit for saving your brother."

Theo sat down next to Francie and put his arm around her. "She was a real hero," he agreed. "When she wasn't being a complete weasel."

A kind of snorting guffaw escaped Francie. Theo laughed, too. But in the next instant, she was crying.

"You've had a day of it," the sheriff said, getting up. "But you're going to have to come with me."

26
ALMOST CHRISTMAS

BECAUSE OF A THAW, followed by rain, there hadn't been much to do at the skating rink where Francie had been assigned community service. A couple of weeks had passed since the fateful day in the fish house. She'd had to appear in court, and now she was fulfilling her court-ordered community service obligations. She didn't complain. She knew she was lucky and had gotten a lenient sentence after she confessed to tampering with a crime scene and withholding information from law enforcement.

She and Buck swept out the warming shack, emptied the trash, and chipped away at ancient chewing gum under the benches. While they picked up litter outside, they talked about what they were going to do after graduation—provided they graduated.

Buck wanted to get a job where he could earn enough money to buy a GMC half-ton truck. "Maybe if they get that mine going," he said.

Francie spun on him. "That's a terrible idea," she said.

"Why? They've been mining up here for a hundred years." Buck stabbed a flattened takeout carton with his trash picker.

"Sure, iron mining," Francie said. "That's a lot different. Copper-nickel mining creates so much toxic material—sulfuric acid, arsenic, lead—and that's just for starters. All of that could have a devastating effect on the watershed. Anyway, most mining jobs are or will be automated. Once the mine closes, which it will, most of the money goes into the pockets of a giant multinational corporation, not to the people who live here. The lakes are poisoned. And you're out of a job."

"Well, you're Little Miss Sunshine," Buck grumbled, trying to extricate the litter from the sharp end of his trash picker.

"Why don't you go to college and get a teaching degree?" Francie said in a rush. "You'd be a great elementary ed teacher. I've seen how you handle the kids on the rink. They look up to you. You're fair. You're kind to the kids who are bullied and firm with the bullies. Firm, but kind. You seem to understand them."

"Well, I'll think about it," he said. He twisted his garbage bag shut, smiling, and said, "What about you?"

Francie didn't know. It was getting pretty late for college applications, she supposed. What she didn't tell Buck was that her life felt pretty unsettled. Worse than unsettled. She'd gotten herself into trouble in school, trouble with the law, with her granddad, and for what? She was no closer to finding her mom. And worse, she was in possession of something so rare and so valuable that some people were willing to do almost anything to get it. So she was also afraid.

She stopped picking up trash for a minute and patted the inside zipper pocket of her jacket, feeling for the tiny packet she carried with her everywhere. It was something she did a million times a day, just to make sure she still had it.

Thanks, Aunt Astrid, for the lesson in sleight of hand, Francie thought. Her little ruse—putting jelly beans in the box before closing it up——seemed to have convinced Boris and Tire Tread that the seeds were inside. Had the box gone to the bottom of the lake, or had the thugs fished it out and taken it with them? Francie and Theo hadn't waited to find out.

Later at home, she sat staring at the small packet on her kitchen table. *If only I could remember more about what happened to my mother. If I could, would it help me to find her?*

What if, she wondered. *What if I opened the packet and ate a seed? Just one. Would that help me remember where Mom had gone that fateful day?* Maybe her mother had told Francie something important, and she had forgotten it.

She turned the packet in her fingers, wondering. Would it take one seed? More? Would she have to eat them all to feel any effect? What if the seeds did nothing and it was the plant itself that had memory-enhancing properties? The flower? The leaves?

She didn't know, and the only person she knew who might—the plant collector—was dead.

Except. Except . . . what about Loretta? Francie knew that she had first encountered the box at Loretta's cabin. What kind of a connection to the box, to the seeds, to this whole mystery did Loretta have? And if she did know about the seeds, that they were said to restore memory, couldn't she have cured herself? She must have known something, because she had that bookmark.

Francie resolved that if she didn't make any progress on finding her mother by Christmas, she was going to try drastic measures. She was going to try eating one or more seeds.

But then, just before Christmas, Francie came home from her duties at the skating rink to find a letter waiting for her.

Tucked in among the bills, junk mail, and flyers was a plain white envelope without a stamp, no address—not even her name on the front. As she slit the envelope with a knife, Francie expected to find an offer for a low-interest credit card or pizza coupons, but it was a typed note. Very simple, it read:

The time has come. Meet me at Loretta's cabin on Christmas Day. Come alone—I want to see you—just you—for a little while before we go surprise the others. All will be explained. Until then, yours forever, your mother. And her signature.

Francie lowered herself onto a chair and set the note on her lap. She took a deep breath. Waited for her heart to settle.

What if this was a trick? What if the letter wasn't from her mother? She felt ashamed of doubting her own mother, but why would her mother tell her to come alone? That was weird. Suspicious, even.

But there was her signature. And hadn't Boris hinted that she was nearby?

No. She shouldn't buy this. It seemed fishy. She should show it to the police—or at least to Theo.

On the other hand, what if it was from her mother? If she showed it to Theo, he would insist on coming with her, and that was not what her mother had wanted. Her mother? She was already thinking of the letter as if it was from her mother. *Which she shouldn't do!* she scolded herself.

But what if it was?

Francie resolved that she would show Theo the letter. After all, hadn't it been her mother who had warned her not to trust anyone? But he wasn't around. He had gone to warm up the cabin and prepare a Christmas Eve meal for everyone. Christmas Eve was the next day.

Well, she thought, she'd tell him when she got out there.

The next day she picked up the aunts and Granddad from the hotel where they had been staying and drove out to Sandy's resort. Sandy had agreed to take them across the now-frozen bay by snowmobile, which he did by twos, one person on the back and another in the sled behind.

"Is the ice safe?" Francie asked, wondering if she would ever get over her fear of being on ice again.

Sandy explained the route he'd take across the lake. "Don't worry," he said solemnly, before handing Francie a helmet and then donning his own. "The ice is good and thick, at least on this bay. Over there," he waved his hand vaguely toward the wider part of the lake, "there's weak ice, but don't worry—we're not going anywhere near it."

Once all the gear and food and presents had been lugged up to the cabin with Sandy's help, he waved goodbye, toting off a couple of jars of prickly pear jam from the aunts and a big fat tip from Granddad.

Theo announced that he was going to go cut a tree, and at first Francie thought that might be a good time to confide in him, but the aunts wanted help making up the beds, so she stayed behind to do that.

When Theo returned, there was the tree to put up and preparations for the meal and gifts to wrap. Theo spent most of his time in the kitchen, cooking. And still no time to talk to him alone, with the aunts buzzing around him like bees around honey.

Francie felt constantly chilled. She kept piling on more sweaters and wrapping scarves around her neck, as if being warm would tamp down the anxiety she felt as she mulled over what to do.

Maybe she could talk to Theo while they set the table for dinner, Francie thought as she pulled silverware from the closed-up—and cold—drawer. Her damp fingers stuck to the ice-cold metal utensils.

"Aahh!" she squealed, holding up her hand. A fork and knife clung to her fingers as if they were magnetic.

Theo laughed, grabbed her arm, dragged her to the sink, and stuck her hand in the dishpan where the utensils fell off in the warm water.

Now, Francie thought. Now I'll tell him. "Theo," she said.

But something on the stove started smoking and the smell of burning onions permeated the air. Theo raced outside carrying the smoking pan and tossed it, steaming, into the snow.

Then there was dinner and after dinner they gathered around the tree, lit with candles, which Granddad complained loudly about. "Gonna burn the place down!" he squawked as they were lit. They sang a few wobbly carols, blew out the candles to placate Granddad, and got down to opening their presents.

Francie tried to get into the festive mood, but the letter and what she should do and her mother and the morning and whether she should tell anybody all churned around inside her and finally settled like a lump of cold mashed potatoes in her belly.

She barely paid attention while the others unwrapped their presents. Theo had found silk scarves for the aunts, a wool one for Granddad, and for Francie, a Swiss Army knife.

"Thanks," Francie said, making a show of inspecting all the gizmos, including three different blades, a file, a toothpick, a tweezers, and a corkscrew.

"Every woodswoman needs one," Theo said.

"A corkscrew?" Aunt Jeannette asked. "What does she need that for?"

"That's in case *you* need one, Auntie," Theo said.

Francie was quiet, not joining in on the teasing, and Astrid leaned over, patted her hand, and said, "You're thinking about your mother, aren't you?" Of course she was, although probably not the way her aunt thought she was. Francie nodded, blinking back tears.

After they had opened all their gifts there were still two boxes under the tree from Granddad to Francie and Theo. But instead of handing them the boxes, Granddad stood up, clapped his hands, and said, "You'll have to go outside to find your gifts from me."

Francie and Theo looked at each other with surprise, went to the door, slid into their boots, and stepped outside.

There, stuck into the snow in front of the door, were two pairs of very skinny-looking skis and two pairs of poles.

"They're for cross-country skiing," Granddad explained. "The boots are in the boxes under the tree."

"But how did you get the skis here without us seeing?" Francie asked.

"A little help from Sandy," Granddad said.

So that, Francie thought, explained the big tip.

Now it was morning—Christmas morning—and the whole night had gone by without saying anything to anybody about the letter. She still had to decide if she was going to trust that it was from her mother or not. If she was going to get up right now when everyone was sleeping and creep outside or if she should wake Theo and tell him everything.

She rose on one elbow to look out the window, but it was so covered with frost—a fairyland of icy ferns—she couldn't see out of it. The picture of the skis leaning against the cabin came to her. Maybe she would go out and just give them a try—not to go anywhere, just to try the skis. That way, when she and Theo went out a little later, she'd be better at it than he was.

That was a good enough reason to not wake him, so she got up, pulled on long johns, lined wind pants, and climbed down the ladder from the loft. She slid into her new ski boots—so much lighter than downhill boots—and as quietly as she could, slipped into her noisy down jacket. She put her phone in one pocket and her new pocketknife in the other, then patted the inside zipper pocket to reassure herself the seeds were still there. Plunked hat on head, shoved mitts on hands, and stepped outside, closing the door very quietly behind her.

The world was fresh and new, every branch and twig sparkling with snow.

Was she the fairy-tale princess about to set off on a quest into the enchanted forest, she wondered, as she stepped out into the glittering world? It was possible, she knew, that there might be trolls to be slain.

The cold penetrated every little weak spot in her clothing, sneaking under her collar, along the zipper of her jacket, prying into the space between her mittens and her sleeves. It pricked at her face, and she kept her mouth tightly closed over her teeth lest they crack from the cold. It felt like everything might crack: teeth, bones, buttons, the soles of her boots.

The skis, which she plucked up from where they leaned against the side of the cabin, were skinnier and much lighter than downhill skis. And she found out once she got the boots clicked into the bindings . . . so much slipperier! The skis seemed to take off, leaving her and her behind in the snow.

She picked herself up, dusted the snow off her rear, and got her poles planted, then took a few tentative strides, hoping her fingers would warm up the way they had when she'd been snowshoeing with Raven.

Just a little skiing practice, she told herself, and then she'd go tell Theo about the letter, and together they'd decide what to do. But she found herself gliding along easily. The earlier thaw and then a hard freeze had formed a hard crust on top of the deep snow. Walking, she'd likely break through the crust, but on skis she was able to float on top, and a fresh dusting of snow made for soft, buttery skiing.

"Kick and glide" is what Theo had said you were supposed to do in this kind of skiing. So she tried, reminding herself to *kick and glide, kick and glide* as she went along. In very little time, she had come to the jack pine forest where Raven said there were blueberry bushes under the snow.

Probably, Francie thought, her mother just wanted a chance to explain to Francie why she had left her as a young child at Loretta's. That must be it. Francie would go to Loretta's and have a wonderful reunion with her mother full of hugs and tears and apologies. Then the two of them would go back to the aunts' cabin and have a lovely Christmas dinner with the whole family.

She had been the last to see her mother and now she would be the first. Now it made sense. She knew what she was doing. She was headed to the cabin by herself, as she probably knew she would all along.

Kick and glide, kick and glide, Francie went along, warming up as she had hoped she would. With the neck gaiter over her mouth and nose, even the tip of her nose was warm.

In a kind of movie-montage sort of way, Francie began to imagine the life she and her mother would have. She saw them swinging shopping bags on a sunny city street, laughing over lunch in a fancy restaurant, heads thrown back with glee on a roller coaster, eating sticky wands of cotton candy, and late-night pajama party snuggles in a big, comfy bed.

This is what she was thinking when she caught a glimpse of the wolf. The same wolf she'd seen before—the one she'd thought of as the queen. Farther away than before but still close enough to see her frosty whiskers and her breath like a wisp of smoke from her mouth. This time, the wolf wasted no time in bolting straight off into the woods. Francie stood for a few moments, feeling a combination of wondrous admiration and gut-squeezing fear.

Was it an omen of some sort? Good? Or bad? Should she go back or continue on?

She went on, committed. Committed to the journey. As committed to her hunt as the wolf was to hers.

27
LORETTA'S CABIN

Even before Loretta's cabin came into view, she smelled wood smoke and as she grew closer saw a curl of smoke rising from the chimney.

Someone was here.

Francie felt a little sick. Maybe because she hadn't eaten breakfast, but maybe from sudden anxiety. She felt her aloneness, her vulnerability. What had she been thinking? Of course it was a trap. Why, oh why hadn't she told Theo?

Instead, she had come here, just like whoever had written her that letter wanted her to, all alone, without telling anyone where she was going. Stupid! Stupid! Stupid!

Now what was she going to do? The smart thing would be to turn around and ski home as fast as she could. Or maybe she could make a call. She pulled her phone out of her pocket.

No service. Battery nearly dead. Oh yeah, *cold*. Phones hated that.

She could turn around right now and ski back to the aunts' cabin, get help, call the sheriff.

But what if it was nothing? Just some cold hunter warming up? She'd look dumb. And she hardly wanted to draw attention to herself after the kind of trouble she'd already gotten into with the sheriff.

So before heading home, she could at least try to figure out who was inside.

All the windows facing her were boarded up, but around the other side, where she and Raven had kicked out the plywood, there was one window through which she would be able to see—and be seen, she reminded herself, so she'd have to be careful.

She left her skis and poles at the edge of the forest and crept around the cabin to the other side. Then she edged slowly, slowly up to the window and peeked inside.

A quick glance around the inside of the cabin revealed only one person. This person—a woman—was bent over, shoving a stick of wood into the woodstove. Francie needed only to see the back of her head, with hair like Francie's, but threaded with silver, like little stars in a dark sky, and the white streak like the Milky Way. Her mother.

Clues. Her mother had left her clues, she knew now. The footprints by the aunts' cabin. The lipstick in her apartment. Her mother had stayed here, in this cabin. That's why there had been blankets here and warm embers in the woodstove.

Francie wanted to think her mother had been keeping an eye on her. She wanted to believe she'd been here all along, watching out for her daughter. But then where had she been when Theo was kidnapped? Why had she let Francie walk into danger? Why hadn't she herself come to Theo's rescue?

These thoughts passed through Francie's mind in an instant. In the same moment, her mother turned toward the window and saw her daughter. Francie watched her mother's features change from surprise to dismay to what looked a lot like anger.

Francie turned away from the window and ran around the side of the cabin, just in time to see the door fly open and her mother appear.

"Are those your skis?" was the first thing out of her mouth. She pointed to the skis left in the snow at the edge of the woods.

A little stunned by the question, Francie turned to look at them. "Yes," she answered and was turning back to ask why, but her mother spoke first.

"Put them back on and get out of here," she demanded.

"You told me to come!"

"What?" Iris said.

"I got a letter—from you—saying to meet you at Loretta's today."

"No." Iris shook her head. "No," she repeated. "You need to get out of here right away. Can you find your way to your aunts' cabin?"

"Of course I can!" Francie said, bristling. "I got here, didn't I?"

"Good," Iris said, turning away. "Go there—*now*!"

Iris retreated into Loretta's cabin, and Francie stood staring after her, wondering what that was all about. After all this time, and this is how her mother greeted her? She kicked at the snow, then stared at the cabin door, hoping her mother would reappear and they could try their greeting again and do it better this time. But the door stayed shut. Her mother clearly didn't want to talk to her.

So much for cotton candy and pajama parties, Francie thought as she stomped away cursing under her breath, then not under her breath. Why had her mother been so angry? Or had it been some other emotion—not anger? A troubling feeling played at the edges of Francie's consciousness as she picked up her skis and turned them around so they faced the direction she was supposed to go.

With a sigh, she stepped into her ski bindings. But she couldn't get the toe of her boot to snap into the binding the way it was supposed to. She tried jamming the toe in harder but it didn't work. Again and again she tried, but it was no use. Finally examining the ski, she could see that snow and ice had built up in the binding, so she slipped off her mitten and dug at it with her fingers until they grew so bone-achingly cold she couldn't stand it—which took about three seconds—so she slid her mitten back on and once again just tried jamming her boot into the binding again. This time her ski slipped out from under her and she fell flat on her face. The deep snow that broke her fall also worked its way into her mittens, down the neck of her jacket, and coated her face like a shaving-cream pie.

She was ready to just lie there and bawl like a baby when she felt a hand grasp her arm and pull her upright. Looking up, she saw through the melting snow and her tears that it was not her mother, as she hoped. It was a man.

She was too surprised to even speak.

"You okay?" he asked, his voice full of concern. His stocking cap was pulled down to his eyebrows and the hood of his parka pulled up over his cap, but what she could see of his face was sort of familiar. His voice, too. But she couldn't quite place him.

"Yeah, sure," she said. She pulled off her wet mitten and wiped the snow off her face. "Just clumsy."

"I don't mean to pry, but are you okay? Anything I can do to help?"

"No, I'm fine." Francie tucked her frozen hands under her armpits to warm them up. "Just having a little trouble with my skis."

Where had this guy come from? she wondered as he picked up her skis and brushed the snow off them. Should she be worried? He leaned the skis against a tree while Francie wondered if her mother was having some kind of affair with this guy. That would explain what he was doing here and why her mother had been so anxious to get rid of Francie.

"The bindings might ice up if you leave them in the snow like that," he explained, picking up her poles and leaning them also against the tree.

"The bindings *are* iced up," she said.

"Maybe you should take them into the cabin and get them thawed out." He took the skis and started walking toward the cabin. "You, too. You look positively frozen."

Her hands and fingers were aching with cold, and she was losing feeling in her toes. "Okay," she said and jogged toward the cabin thinking, *This should be interesting.* Just how would her mother react to Francie returning with her mother's boyfriend?

But the cabin was empty. Her mother wasn't there.

"Mom?" Francie poked her head behind the curtain between the main room and the tiny bedroom, but there was no one there. And the rest of the cabin could be seen with a swivel of the head. "Where's my mom?" she said to the man who had entered behind her and was leaning the skis against the wall.

"Oh, was your mother here?" he asked, as he carefully brushed every speck of snow off the skis.

"I just talked to her!" Francie said, gazing all around the cabin as if she might have missed seeing her somehow. Her glance fell on the closet where she and Raven had hidden—but why would her mother be in there?

"Maybe she went out?" the man said. "To get wood? Or to the outhouse?"

Wouldn't Francie have seen her if she'd left the cabin? Well, she *had* gotten distracted by the whole ski binding fiasco. She supposed it was possible. And the fact that her mother hadn't helped her when she was struggling with her skis just felt like a little knife twist in her gut.

Or maybe that little knife twist was from something else, she thought, suddenly realizing she was alone in this cabin with a man she didn't really know at all. It had seemed fine when she thought her mother was here, but now it was odd. The whole thing was starting to feel stomach-churningly strange. Like, where had this guy even come from? And why hadn't she asked him that while they were still outside?

"I should go," Francie said.

"Oh, I see you're worried," he said. "Don't be! Look, you go warm up by the woodstove over there, and I'll stay right over here. I just don't want to be responsible for you freezing to death out there!" He smiled and nodded at the woodstove.

He had a point. She could grab her skis and go, but then she'd be out in the bone-chilling cold with half-frozen hands and feet. And frozen ski bindings. If he had wanted to harm her, he'd had plenty of opportunity already. And she supposed she was panicking about her mom for nothing. She would probably come bursting in with an armload of wood any moment.

So Francie stood by the woodstove and tried not to worry, watching as the man flipped back the hood of his jacket and pulled off his hat.

"Wait a minute," she said. "I know you. You were at the skating rink."

"That's right," the man said.

"What did you say your name was?"

"Louis Streife," he said. "You can call me Lou."

Oh, yeah, loosestrife, like the invasive species. "You must have given Loretta a card at one time," she said slowly, remembering. "I found it here, at this cabin." She didn't add that it had been in the kindling bucket with other scraps of paper to be burned.

"Oh, yes!" he said. "I guess I did! Ha. What a good memory you have. My my."

"What is the name of your business again?"

"Glentech."

"Pharmaceuticals," Francie added, remembering Jay's research. "You left your card in the door of my apartment."

"Yes," he said. "It's too bad you didn't contact me back then. Maybe things wouldn't have had to progress to the point that they have."

"What?" Francie said, feeling that little knife make another painful twist in her gut. "What do you mean?"

"I think you may have come into possession of something I've been trying to procure for a very long time," he said. "I traced it to this cabin, when your friend Loretta lived here."

Francie did not want to think about why her heart was clattering away like a room full of rhythm-challenged tap dancers as she said, "So that must have been before the accident that sent her to the nursing home."

"Quite so." He sounded not one bit sorry when he added, "Bad luck."

Bad luck? Francie wondered. Or had it been something more sinister? Dots started to connect in her head. The "gentleman" that Miss Schell had told Buck was interested in the box. Maybe that gentleman had been this gentleman.

"What went wrong at the museum?" she wondered, realizing too late she had wondered it out loud.

"That curator was a sour old lady, wanting way too much money, saying she had decided to have the box assessed. When I pressed her a little, she said she'd hidden it where no one would ever find it. I must have lost my temper," Lou said, smiling.

This time she saw through the fake warmth in his smile to the bone-chilling soul at its core. "It was just unlucky for her that the knife was right there, handy. I think I showed restraint by not killing her."

"The plant collector, Mr. Skitterly, wasn't so lucky," Francie said, watching as he slipped off his mittens, revealing gloved hands beneath. She crammed her own hands into her jacket pockets and felt the smooth, reassuring contours of the knife Theo had given her. Could she protect herself with a little pocket-knife? The blades were all still tucked securely in their slots. How could she get one of them open without being noticed?

As she felt along the blades of the knife with one hand, she said, "And who better than a pharmaceutical chemist to concoct a poison to mimic a plant collector's poisonous plant?"

"Oh, I'm not a chemist," he said. "And anyway, I didn't need to concoct anything! The poisons were right there! Handy. One could hardly help oneself." He chuckled at the memory.

Her next question made Francie tremble in the very core of her being, but she had to ask, "And just where is my mother right now?" She tried to keep her voice level, not crying, not giving in to the utter terror she was really feeling.

"She's having a little nap," the man whispered as if talking about a baby in the next room. He tilted his head toward the closet.

"A nap," Francie croaked, moving toward the closet door.

The man stepped in front of it and held up a finger. "Shhh!" he said. "Mustn't wake her!"

The knife in her gut twisted and twisted. Inside her pocket her fingers pinched and pried, trying to pull a blade from the knife. Again and again, her fingers failed her.

"What do you want?" she said, stepping away from him.

"For far too long I thought it was your mother who was keeping the box from me. Then I learned she had left it with some old herbalist back in the woods, but I arrived to find the old

woman had 'gotten rid of it,' so she said. Then it went from hand
to hand, none of these hands realizing what they possessed. At
last, things came together. Your mother was back in the neigh-
borhood, the box was back in play, it must be in your mother's
hands again, I thought. But no, it was not."

Francie had not succeeded in pulling a blade out of the knife.
The only thing she could pry loose with one hand was the corkscrew. A corkscrew did not seem like an effective weapon.

"No," Lou continued, "it was not in your mother's hands. It
was in your hands, then your brother's . . ."

Now, she thought, run at him and stab him. But how likely
was it that she could mortally wound him with a corkscrew? He'd
probably just take the knife away from her and use it against her.

Keep him talking, she thought, so she said, "Well, the box
is . . ."

"On the bottom of the lake," he finished her sentence.

Okay, Francie thought, so he knows that. So why did he lure
me here?

"I see you're thinking away over there," he said. "Let's just
cut to the chase, shall we?" he proposed. "I believe that you still
possess what was inside the box."

Francie was stunned. A whole percussion section started
banging away inside her chest: kettledrums, snare drums, con-
gas, even a jingling tambourine. "The box was empty," she managed to choke out.

"You know it wasn't."

Was he bluffing? Or did he really know?

"Maybe your henchmen have what you're looking for?" she
suggested.

"Henchmen?"

"Boris and Tire Tread. Aren't they working for you?"

"Boris and Tire Tread?" he asked, at first confused, then he threw back his head and laughed. "Yes, I see where you get those names. Very funny! But you're barking up the wrong subsidiary. Those two are not the sharpest tools in the shed. Keeping the seeds for themselves would be well beyond the scope of their wit. No, I think *you're* the clever one. You're the one who, with some sleight of hand, managed to spirit the seeds away and you still possess them, and if you want to help your mother, you'll give them to me."

"Well, I don't have them on me!" Francie lied. "And I'm not saying anything more until I know my mother is alive."

"Well, fine," Lou said. He opened the door to the closet and Francie swallowed hard when she saw her mother slumped inside, leaning sideways against the wall, head hanging, chin almost on chest, her hands behind her back.

"There," he said.

"I have to make sure she's breathing," Francie said and pushed past him into the closet. He didn't stop her, and for a moment she wondered if he'd slam the door on both of them, but he just stood, leaning against the door frame, watching her.

Francie knelt down next to her mother and gently smoothed the hair away from her face—as if that was going to do any good! Then she noticed her mother's wrists were bound behind her back.

"You've tied her hands!" Francie cried. "Why? I mean, why would you need to do that? She's out cold!"

"Well, not forever!" he said. "She'll have to wake up sometime."

Francie found some reassurance in that, and in seeing the rise and fall of her mother's chest. Still, she pressed her head to it. Hearing her mother's heartbeat steadied her. It gave her just enough mental space to think, and what came to mind was the knife in her pocket and what use it could be put to. The worst

Francie would be able to do with it would be to poke a hole in Lou and enrage him, like a wounded bear.

So instead, she shifted her position as if she just wanted to get more comfortable, then managed, without Lou seeing her, to sneak the knife out of her pocket, flip open one of the blades, and place the knife in her mother's hands.

When she noticed one of those hands curling around the knife, Francie felt a shiver of hope. Her mother was not as unconscious as she'd thought!

"Hey, now, what are you doing?" Lou grabbed Francie's arm and yanked her out of the closet and slammed the door shut. Francie twisted out of his grip and skittered backward, hoping she was getting somewhere near her skis.

"You've been playing around with something in that pocket this whole time," he said. "I think you have the seeds on you!" He plunged his free hand into her pocket, which had until recently held the knife, and said, "Where are they? I know you have them!"

"You can see I don't!" she said as she backed away, catching a glimpse of her skis within arm's reach. "Do you think I carry them around or something?"

She reached for her ski poles just as Lou lunged toward her. But a noise from the closet made him turn. That was all the time she needed to swing the poles at his neck. He must have seen them coming, because he ducked, but too late—the poles cracked him on the side of the head and he winced, clutching his head in his hands and letting out a string of colorful cuss words.

Before he recovered from the crack on the skull, she whipped the poles at him again, this time catching him in the shins. He yowled, spewing ever more elaborate curses as he hobbled toward her. She got in a swift kick to his groin, grabbed her skis, and charged out the door.

Once outside, she threw her skis in the snow and stepped into the bindings. Her boots clicked into place with a satisfying *click*, *click*, just as Lou lunged out the door after her. But she glided away, purposely heading for the heavily crusted snow in the woods.

"Come back here if you ever want to see your mother alive again!" he shouted after her.

Francie hesitated and, turning back, saw her mother staggering out the open door onto the stoop, the knife in her hands.

Iris squinted in the snow-bright day like someone who had just woken up from a drunken—in this case more likely drugged—stupor. She pointed the blade at Lou and said, "Let her go." Her words slurred a little as she added, "This is between you and me."

There was no way she was in any condition to stand up to anyone, especially with a Swiss Army knife her only weapon.

"Lou!" Francie called to him. "I lied. I *do* have the seeds. If you want them, you'll have to come and get them."

He moved toward her, but as soon as he left the hard-packed path, first one foot and then the other plunged through the crust, and he wallowed knee-deep in the snow.

"Come on, Lou," Francie called.

"Don't listen to her," Iris said. "I'm the only one who knows where the seeds really are."

"They're on me!" Francie said. "I've got them right here."

Lou looked from one to the other—Iris standing in the doorway, weaving slightly, her hair flying in wild strands around her face; Francie poised like a jackrabbit, ready to spring away. If Lou went for her mother, Francie would go back. Iris was in no condition to put up a fight against anyone.

Instead, he pulled himself out of the snow and once back on

the hard-packed path ran away from both of them. Francie almost laughed, except, following his movement, she caught the glint of something shiny and blue hidden among the trees.

The distinctive sputtering growl of a snowmobile engine sent her skittering away through the woods as fast as she could go. Well, she thought, she had wanted him to follow her, maybe not on a snowmobile, but at least it meant he was leaving her mother alone.

Kick and glide, kick and glide, she reminded herself, but it was more like *slip, slide, fall on her butt, stumble up, slip, fall, pick herself up.* Even on the hard crust where she had the advantage, she broke through now and then.

So she went for the narrow deer paths that twisted through the thick brush, too narrow for a machine, almost too narrow for her. Clambering over fallen trees or crashing through brush or negotiating the hummocky ground of a bog, she tried to go where a snowmobile couldn't. Still, she could hear the whine of the machine, sometimes sounding uncomfortably close, sometimes far away. But if she paused at all and listened, she could almost always hear it.

"If you feel endangered, make your way to a public place and call law enforcement," her granddad had told her. The closest and only place was the aunts' cabin. Where there were people and working phones. She should be there soon, she was pretty sure.

But when she finally emerged from a deer path into a clearing, it wasn't the aunts' cabin she had come to, but the bare expanse of a frozen lake.

She skied down the cleared slope to the shore and peered out. It had to be Enchantment Lake. But *where* on the lake? It all looked so unfamiliar and disorienting. Ah, but there, across the lake, where the land curved like a sheltering arm around the water: one lone cabin with windows aglow with light, a lovely warm curl of smoke rising from the chimney. Home.

She could ski around the edge of the lake, hugging the shore, to reach it. That would be the safest but the slowest. Which made it not the safest. The fastest way would be to cut across the frozen lake. Also not safe. But at least fast.

Did she dare, though? Was she brave enough to venture out onto the ice like that? As she stood, trying to decide, the ice—or the restless water beneath, Francie wasn't exactly sure—rumbled and moaned like a giant rolling over, groaning in his sleep.

The whine of the snowmobile somewhere in the woods sent her leaping forward, still with pounding heart and aching lungs, onto the ice.

28

THE GIANT UNDER THE ICE

Kick and glide, kick and glide. She kept her eyes on the cabin on the far shore and wondered what the others were doing right then. They probably assumed she was still fast asleep in the loft. The aunts would be tiptoeing around in the kitchen, whispering, trying not to wake her. Theo would be stoking the fire, and Granddad probably grousing about not having a newspaper to read. The cabin would be fragrant with cinnamon rolls and coffee, and soon the rolls would come out of the oven, warm and gooey, and the aunts would call up to the loft telling Francie that breakfast was ready.

How long before Theo climbed the ladder and discovered she was not there? The very last place they would expect to see her would be skiing across the lake toward the cabin. But if they looked out the window, they might see her, although soon she would be hidden by the island that stood between her and the cabin.

Her legs and arms ached. Her lungs burned from the effort

of gasping in the frigid air. She did not know if she could go on. Just as far as the island, she thought, then she could rest.

But the sudden growl of the snowmobile as it charged out of the woods shot her through with a new burst of adrenaline. After a quick glance over her shoulder, she knew she had neither time nor breath to even curse. She could only keep going, kicking and gliding, murmuring, *Far, far away there is a lake,* to keep up her rhythm. *On the lake is an island,* to keep up her courage. *On the island is a church,* to keep up hope. *In the church is a well,* to keep breathing. *In the well swims a duck,* to keep going. *In the duck is an egg,* to keep believing. *In the egg is my heart!* to keep telling herself that she had found her mother. She had really found her mother.

The snowmobile was gaining on her. She didn't have to look— she could hear it getting closer and closer. How far away was the cabin? Impossibly far. But what could she do? There was only one way to get there—*kick and glide, kick and glide.*

Until her skis stopped cooperating. Suddenly, her skis just . . . stuck. The snow looked the same as everywhere else: pristine, white, and pure. But the minute her ski sank a millimeter into it, the snow turned to slush and the slush instantly turned to ice on the bottom of her skis. It was like trying to ski on Velcro.

Kick and glide turned into a Frankenstein-like clomp, clomp, clomp. More and more slush froze and stuck to the bottom of her skis until they became like platform shoes.

She just kept clomping along as the sound of the snowmobile grew closer and closer. Lou yelled angrily at her—she didn't know what. She couldn't hear over the sound of her own breathing and clomping. All she knew was that the snowmobile was almost upon her.

In fairy tales, the young, not overly bright hero usually

stumbled onto success. Like the fairy-tale heroines she had read about in her mother's book, she wished she had a magic comb to throw behind her that would turn into a forest of trees, or a mirror that tossed behind her would transform into a vast lake. And then she realized that she did have something she could throw behind her, something that would slow her pursuer down. Even make him stop.

She pulled the packet of seeds from her inside pocket, stopped, turned, and waved it high in the air so he could see the copper-colored packet flashing in the sun.

"Here they are. Here they are!" she said and threw them as far away from her as she could, which was not nearly far enough.

But what was done was done, and she couldn't change it now, so she turned and clomped away. Lou's hollering became angrier and angrier, until it was a crazy, high-pitched scream, even as she heard the snowmobile slow, then sputter, then die.

And then there was nothing. No growl of snowmobile. No yelling or screaming. Just the rolling, watery, booming roar of the giant under the ice.

Francie looked over her shoulder expecting to see Lou sneaking up on her. But no, there was nothing. No Lou, no snowmobile. There was only, Francie was terrified to see, an expanding pool of open water—and water sloshing up over the broken edges of the ice, reaching almost to her skis.

29

LATER THAT SAME NIGHT

FRANCIE WASN'T ENTIRELY SURE how she got back to the cabin (had Sandy come to her rescue?), because shortly after returning to her aunts' warm cabin, she had fallen into a sleep of oblivion.

She was awakened much later and called to the table where a Christmas feast of roast goose, wild rice, and dozens of side dishes awaited. Around the table sat her aunts, Theo, Sandy, Sandy's mom, and, most miraculous of all, her mother. Her own mother, right there, at the table!

Francie should have been, at the very least, happy. But the thrill of having her mother sitting across from her was tempered by the memory of what had happened on the ice earlier that day. She had led a man to his death! On top of that, she, Francie, had thrown away the miracle-working seeds—thrown them away! Seeds so significant that her mother had faked her own death to protect them.

And now her mother smiled at Francie while passing the

lingonberry sauce. How would Francie ever be able to tell her mother what she had done? That in a panicked bid to save her own skin, she'd thrown away the seeds—for no good reason! The fact that she hadn't known that the ice would give way right then gave her no solace. She was miserable and exhausted. Shortly after dinner she climbed the ladder to the loft and crawled into bed.

Later, she heard the peculiar creaking of the loft ladder and smelled the still unfamiliar but now identifiable scent of her mother and felt her weight on the mattress as she sat down. Next, her mother's hand on her hair. Francie pretended to be asleep but had to nearly hold her breath in order to hear her mother's soft words.

"Franny? Are you sleeping?"

Francie pretended that she was.

"You have every right to be angry with me," her mother whispered. "It was wrong of me to leave you for so long. Some-day I will try to tell the whole story, and I hope you'll be able to forgive me."

Francie felt tears coming to her eyes and thought, *No no, if I start crying, she'll know I'm listening. And then I'll need to confess what I did.* So she kept still and did not sniff when her nose started to run.

"I'm sorry to have missed so much of your life," her mother went on. "You've grown into an amazing young woman. So brave! Such heart! I couldn't be more proud of you."

Francie just barely managed to hold back the sob rising in her throat, only releasing it after she heard her mother retreat back down the loft ladder. She felt a jumble of emotions. Relief. At long last, her mother! Anger. Why had their mother left them for so long? Was that really necessary? And these feelings were overlaid with an immense and overriding sense of guilt: she had thrown away the seeds but was too ashamed to admit it.

She would have to talk about it at some point. Tomorrow or the next day—she couldn't pretend to be too tired or traumatized forever. Soon enough the subject would come up. What was she going to say?

30
THE HEART OF THE MATTER

WEEKS WENT BY during which neither mother nor daughter spoke of anything of importance. Francie didn't ask her mother why she had been gone so long because then she knew she would have to explain how she had lost the seeds. Maybe her mother didn't ask Francie about the seeds because then she'd have to explain where she had been all these years. Sometimes Francie felt like they were two wild animals warily circling each other. Who was going to bite the other one first?

Francie and her mother moved into a bigger and nicer apartment while Theo worked on winterizing the cabin. On weekends, mother and daughter went out and helped. Or pretended to. It was nice but strange to have a mother all of a sudden, at age seventeen, just when her classmates were getting ready to leave their parents to go off to college. Francie was used to having a lot of freedom, and she still did. Her mother didn't make rules for her, like you'd expect. But then, Francie was too old to have a set of rules imposed. She would have chafed, and her mom probably knew that. At least that's what Francie told herself.

She tried not to think about what had happened, but of course it weighed on her. She had thrown away the seeds, the thousands-of-years-old, miracle-working seeds, which by now were at the bottom of the lake or in some fish's guts. The weight of her guilt and the weight of their unspoken questions grew heavier and heavier. At last the dam burst and the truth came out, and Francie admitted to her mother what she had done. Then she asked her mother to explain herself—where had she been all these years? And why?

Her mother remained silent for a long moment and then said, "Come on, we're going to go visit Loretta."

The first thing Loretta said when mother and daughter entered her room was, "Did you bring the box?"

Francie and her mother exchanged a glance. Francie had to work around the lump in her throat to explain what had happened, ending with the admission that the box—along with what it contained—was gone forever. Feeling chagrined, Francie set the bookmark on the side table next to Loretta.

Loretta picked it up and gazed at it as if at a photo of an old friend. Then she laughed, which Francie had not been expecting.

"What's so funny?" Francie asked.

"No matter," Loretta said.

"No matter?"

"Of course, as pretty as it was, the box wasn't much," Loretta said. "And the seeds . . ." She giggled so much she had a hard time getting out the rest of the sentence. "They were just poppy seeds!"

"Poppy seeds?" Francie stared at Loretta, dumbfounded.

"The kind you'd use in muffins. I replaced the original ones with poppy seeds."

"So where are the original ones now?"

"The original what, dear?"

"Seeds. The seeds that were in the box."

"Oh, I hid them."

"Hid them where?"

"You know," Loretta said thoughtfully, squinting a bit and peering out the window as if she might see them out there somewhere, "I'm not sure I can remember."

Francie and her mother looked at each other while Loretta gazed out the window. "There used to be a lovely stand of birches right here," she said. "I suppose that's why they call this place Birch Grove. But they cut the birches down to make this place!" She shook her head, then finished with, "Oh yes, now I remember. I remember where I hid them."

Francie leaned forward, waiting for Loretta to tell her what had happened to the seeds. But even at the same time she waited expectantly, Francie felt her heart sinking into her stomach and beyond, continuing toward her feet. Loretta must have hidden them somewhere at her cabin, of course. Where else could it have been? And that cabin had been thoroughly ransacked. True, seeds were small and a packet of seeds might be easily overlooked, but what about mice? Birds? Squirrels? All of whom might have devoured them, buried them, squirreled them away.

"Jelly bean?" Loretta asked, holding the bowl out to her two silently waiting visitors.

"You remembered where you hid the seeds," Francie prompted.

"Oh yes," said Loretta, plucking up a yellow jelly bean for herself. "But nothing can be done until this hip heals."

. . . . .

In the school cafeteria, Francie sat as usual with Raven and Jay. She carefully laid out the lunch she had brought from home: carrot sticks, apple slices, cheese and avocado on homemade bread.

"Nice lunch," Raven said.

"Uh huh," Francie said, hoping Raven would assume that her mother had made it for her.

"You make that yourself?"

"Since when do I make my own lunches?"

Raven looked down at her own uncannily similar lunch and changed the subject. "You doing okay?" she asked.

Francie shrugged.

"I know you're upset about the whole seeds thing, but don't give up hope. You said that Loretta told you that she hid the seeds."

"What's the chance that if she did—*if*—she could ever remember where they were?"

"Stop!" Raven said. "Just stop. Be happy you got your mom— she's alive! You're alive! It could have all gone very differently! Think of it this way: up until this adventure, we didn't even know such a thing as those seeds existed. And we were all fine then!"

"Yeah, you're right," Francie said, picking at the crust of the whole grain bread she'd stayed up until the wee hours making.

Jay slid in next to Francie waving a piece of paper as if it were a flag.

"What's that?" Raven said.

"University of Chicago!" Jay crowed. "Accepted!"

"Wow, Jay, that's great!" Francie said.

"You're going to have to up your joke game," Raven suggested.

"What about you guys? Know where you're going yet?" Jay asked.

Francie pretended her mouth was too full to answer. She pointed at Raven as if to say, You go first.

"I'm going to the tribal college," Raven said.

"That's grand!" Francie exclaimed.

"Sweet!" Jay said. "Got a major figured out yet?"

"No, but ultimately I think I'm interested in environmental law."

"That's perfect!" Francie exclaimed, putting down her sandwich to give a little clap of her hands.

"But, you, Francie," Raven said. "What are you going to do? You gotta do something!"

"Maybe I'll take a year off," Francie said. "So much has happened. Now, finally—a mom! Everyone is so excited to move away from home. Not me."

There was a lot Francie hadn't shared with her friends. Like the fact that having her mother around was more like having a kind of sloppy roommate who left dirty dishes in the sink, wet towels on the floor, didn't make dinner, and slept a lot. A real lot. Her mom had been through some stuff, Francie figured: she probably had about thirteen years of sleep to catch up on.

So Francie shopped and cooked and did the laundry, and her mom seemed to appreciate all of it. They did fun things together when Francie had time—-which wasn't often, because Francie had missed enough school that she had some catching up to do, and finals were coming up, too.

One warm Saturday in May, Francie, Theo, and their mom went to the nursing home to see Loretta. They brought along a loaf of Francie's freshly baked banana bread. Raven came, too. Jay had gone with his parents to Chicago to check out the college he'd be attending in the fall.

Nobody was too surprised to find Granddad was visiting. Loretta and Granddad had struck up quite the friendship during his "undercover" work.

Loretta was standing, looking out the window, watching the birds. After greeting her visitors, and mixing up their names—no surprise—she gestured to the scene outside.

"This used to be woodland," she said. "This time of year it was full of white trillium—so thick sometimes it looked like snow. There was Indian pipe and lots of spring bloomers. Now it's just grass that they have here. They come with a truck and spray chemicals on it and then stick a little sign in the yard that says STAY OFF. Do they think birds know how to read? Do we old folks care if the grass looks like AstroTurf? No. We'd rather see the birds and watch them teach their babies how to get worms out of the ground. After those chemical people are done, the worms are dead. And probably the birds, too." She shook her head.

Francie stared at Loretta, amazed at how clear and cogent she was being. And also sad to think of the birds hunting futilely for bugs and worms to bring to their hatchlings.

Loretta turned to them, smiled, and said, "My hip is healed up. And my mind is much clearer. Let's go!"

"Where are we going?"

"My cabin," Loretta said.

"It's quite a hike in there," Iris said. "Are you sure?"

"You think I don't know how far it is?" Loretta said. "I got this thing." She shook her cane at them, then pointed it at Granddad. "And that fellow to lend me an arm."

On the path to the cabin, the air was scented with every color of green—the fresh-squeezed lime of new buds, the green-pepper scent of ferns, and minty-smelling weeds and wildflowers. The ground was soft and squishy underfoot. Little streams and rivulets sparkled as they made their way from one pond or marsh to another, all the wet spots glowing with bright clumps of yellow marsh marigolds. A high, constant *screee* meant the peepers had hatched, along with a lot of other kinds of croaking, creaking, and chirruping frogs.

As they grew closer to Loretta's cabin, Francie started to think about how the sight of it might affect Loretta. "We should warn you that people have been in your cabin," Francie said.

"It's been fairly well ransacked," Theo added.

Loretta shrugged. "Well, it doesn't matter. It's just stuff."

She didn't seem worried that the seeds might be gone, but Francie couldn't help but be fretful. She and Theo exchanged a glance; he'd been thinking the same thing.

After a while the cabin came into view, and Loretta looked at it a little sadly. "I guess it could use some sprucing up," she said. Then she clapped her hands and said, "But we really aren't going there anyway. Not yet." She veered off into the woods, whacking away at the brush with her cane. The rest of the group stumbled along as best they could, dodging branches, climbing over deadfall, skirting marshy areas. As they went along, Loretta would every so often look down, tap her cane on the ground, and make a little chirping sound.

Finally, after a strenuous twenty minutes, they came into a small clearing, and Loretta stopped. "Well, here you go," she said.

"Here we go what?" Francie asked.

Loretta waved her cane at the ground where small, green plants emerged. It was still too early to tell what they would become, but there was something promising and slightly exotic about their glossy brightness. "This is what became of the seeds," Loretta said.

"These . . . plants?" Francie asked.

"Yep."

"You planted the seeds!"

"Of course I planted them. What else do you do with seeds?"

Francie, Theo, Iris, Granddad, and Raven all stared in wonder at the thickly growing plants that seemed to have sprouted everywhere—even spreading into the nearby forest.

"I planted the first ones very carefully in pots indoors in sterile soil. But when I was quite sure they would thrive here, I looked for an out-of-the-way spot in the woods, hoping those goons from the drug company wouldn't find them," Loretta cackled. "I couldn't picture them tromping back here in their city shoes to look for plants they wouldn't have been able to identify anyway. And they weren't the only ones! That mining company sent somebody, too. I guess they were worried that if some once-believed extinct and highly valuable plant was growing anywhere near where they wanted to mine, that would hold up their permitting process by quite some time." She chuckled. "And I guess it will, because these plants like it here. Even though it took quite a few years to get them established, they've even naturalized and spread a bit."

Francie couldn't help but notice that Loretta seemed suddenly sharp as a tack. Loretta didn't miss Francie's stare, and she reached over and chucked her chin.

"You are such a clever girl I was afraid you were going to see right through me," she said to Francie. Then she turned to Raven and said, "Here's the girl with the eyes that see everything. You knew, didn't you?"

"I only suspected," Raven said.

"Only suspected what?" Francie asked.

"Loretta's memory problems were not all real," Raven explained.

"It was the best way for an old woman to lie low and avoid being hassled by all those goons," Loretta said. "And everyone else who came bothering me. It was effective."

"Well, you fooled me, too," Francie said. "Why didn't you tell me?"

"It was safer for all of us," Loretta explained. "I couldn't really let down my guard at the nursing home, because I was pretty sure someone there was watching me. In fact, when your grand-dad showed up, I thought *he* was the spy!"

"Well," he chuckled, "I *was* watching you. I was watching you to see who else was watching you."

"Yes, I finally figured that out."

"And then I was just keeping an eye on you for the pleasure of it," he said, taking her arm.

Francie and Raven exchanged a wink.

"So there was a spy?" Francie asked as they walked.

"Oh yes," Granddad said. "That aide Marcie. I think she was being paid to keep an eye on Loretta, and to let her employer know who she spoke with and, when possible, what she said."

"Also paid to keep me loopy with drugs, I think," Loretta said.

"That explains why she kept popping into the room when we were there," Francie said. "To find out what we were talking about."

"And to steal my jelly beans!" Loretta crowed.

"And that's how Mr. Streife was able to find out about the box and who had it."

"So what happens now?" Theo asked. "I mean with the plants."

"We let them grow until they make flowers," said Loretta.

"When they go to seed, we collect the seeds. We keep some of the seeds, we plant the rest. They seem to like it here."

They made their way to Loretta's cabin, and after she'd snooped around a bit, they all sat on the stoop outside in the bright sunshine and told the story—or at least some of what had happened nearly fourteen years earlier.

"Your mother and I met long ago, when she was young. And I was a lot younger, too!" Loretta began. "Such an intrepid child she was, to wander so far out into the woods. So we became friends. Of course she grew up and started working, and I saw much less of her."

Iris picked up the thread. "In the course of my work I was assigned a dinosaur-smuggling case—long story—but this led me to other fossil-smuggling activities. During the investigation it was revealed that among long-extinct mastodon and other fossils, some very unusual seeds had been found, but the seeds had mysteriously disappeared before scientists could study them. Of course, smugglers had taken them, but what I realized is that they had been stolen with the help of members of my department, including my superiors. So I located the smugglers, found the stash, and stole the seeds myself. Then I had to disappear, because I was in trouble with everyone."

Loretta went on with the story. "The people who were after Iris threatened harm, not just to her, but to you—her kids—her family. She knew she had to make herself and the seeds disappear, at least for a while. So she came to see me. She brought the seeds and, unexpectedly, her youngest child. That was not part of the plan, but that's what happened. Of course, the seeds couldn't stay viable for long, I knew that! So I planted some right away, as carefully as I could. The others had been well sealed in airtight packets. I had a very complicated puzzle box where I hid the rest of the seeds. Then it occurred to me that I was old, and in case something happened to me, I should show someone how to open the box. So I let you play with it," she said, turning to Francie. "And you know? You figured it out yourself. Almost entirely."

That explained why she'd had a sense of déjà vu when she had opened it this past winter, Francie thought.

"Your mother left and said she hoped to return," Loretta went on, "but if she couldn't, I should return young Franny to her great-aunts' cabin. But I had anticipated a problem. It could endanger everything—the seeds, your mother, even you—if you were to talk about what had transpired. You were only four, so just telling you to keep a secret was not safe enough. I had to make sure you forgot. I am sorry to say that I gave you sleeping herbs so you slept most of the time you were with me. My hope was that if you remembered anything, it would be as hazy as a dream."

"It was," Francie admitted. "And like a dream, I forgot almost all of it."

Iris picked up the story. "I meant to resurface much sooner than now, but once the word got out that I had the seeds, I was pursued by plant collectors—like Skitterly, but others, too, including a variety of shady underworld dealers who recognized the money that could be made. And then there was Glentech and ConiMet and their parent company, Flocore. Rather than becoming less interested in the seeds, Glentech became more interested. When I realized what they wanted to do with them, things became increasingly urgent."

"Why? Didn't they want to gain control of them to have a monopoly?" Theo asked.

"That's what I thought at first," Iris said, "but then I discovered that Streife's plan was not to gain control of the seeds and plants, but to destroy them."

"Why?" Theo asked.

"Glentech was working on developing a synthetic drug that was supposed to enhance memory," Iris went on. "A drug they planned to release in the next couple of years, at thousands of dollars for every injection. The last thing they wanted was a readily available natural product, something people could plant in their own backyards, perhaps! So their plan was to destroy the seeds and any plants that existed—if any did, which Streife suspected. Of course ConiMet, the mining company, wanted to do the exact same thing!"

"Destroy the seeds and any existing plants," Theo said.

"Exactly," Loretta confirmed. "It was important to keep everything secret until enough plants could be propagated and new seed collected to ensure the success of the plants."

"But now it's finally time to turn the enterprise over to the real scientists," Granddad said. "I've been in touch with researchers at the university. This cabin might become a research station." Granddad spun his cane in the air like a soft-shoe dancer.

While the others talked about how that would come to be, Francie leaned against a pine tree and lifted her face to the warm spring sun. Tiny warblers flitted among the balsam branches— little bursts of color among the green boughs, migrants on their way north.

She could never have hoped that everything would turn out quite this well. Maybe not exactly as she had hoped: maybe her mom wasn't the mom she had always imagined, but she was still her mom, and now she was home.

In some ways her mother reminded her of the wolf she had seen not far from here—mysterious and wild. From a daughter's perspective, that wasn't the ideal mother. Yet Francie loved her and, she had to admit, loved her the way she was.

Francie still hadn't written the essay for her college application: Who Am I? That, too, was a mystery. She didn't really know what she wanted to do. Nor did she know what she wanted to be when she grew up, and for sure she didn't know what the future held. She caught a glimpse of it from time to time—like a warbler among the branches—a glimmer of yellow, a streak of red, a hint of something bright and alive and going places.

But she knew she was glad and grateful to be alive in a world where birds flitted among the trees and frogs made a racket and small green plants came out of barely thawed ground. Where wolves still roamed and wilderness still reigned.

Far, far away there is a lake, she thought. *On the shores of the lake there is a forest. In the forest there are trees. In the trees there are birds. In the birds there are songs. And in those songs are stories of thousands of years of wilderness. And in that wilderness, at long last, I have found my heart—among these people, in this forest, on the shores of Enchantment Lake.*

AUTHOR'S NOTE

Although the characters, circumstances, and most of the places in this book are fictional, there are several aspects of the story that are factual.

It is true that scientists successfully germinated plants from seeds five hundred, two thousand, and even thirty-two thousand years old, including a lotus, date palm, and a dainty Siberian flowering plant. These plants were germinated from seeds discovered respectively in a dry lake bed in China, the Israeli desert, and the Siberian permafrost.

It is also true that plants are stolen from state and national parks, public gardens, and private property. In Minnesota, where this story takes place, spruce and balsam boughs and tops, birch bark and saplings, prince's pine, mushrooms, ginseng, blueberries, protected wildflowers, timber, and other plants have been and continue to be illegally harvested from public and private property.

Sulfide ore mining is an ongoing concern in northern Minnesota, where exploration of copper-nickel deposits is taking place. Proponents say mining can be done safely. Others point out that there has not been a single instance of this type of mining that has not caused environmental damage, sometimes catastrophic, and that it is simply too risky in such a water-rich environment.

Although Enchantment Lake and Walpurgis are fictional, two places mentioned in the story are very real and really fine places to visit: the Minneapolis Institute of Art and the Como Park Conservatory. The translucent curtain at the Minneapolis Institute of Art (Mia) that holds Francie's interest, a piece titled *Headwaters* by Minnesota artist Alyssa Baguss, was on temporary exhibit through the Minnesota Artists Exhibition Program at the time I was writing this novel. Another work of art, *Psyche Opening the Golden Box,* by John William Waterhouse, is a real painting, but it is housed in a private collection, not at Mia. The period rooms described in the book (along with others) can be experienced at Mia. The Como Park Conservatory is in St. Paul, Minnesota, adjacent to the Como Park Zoo and a beautiful park and gardens. Visit these amazing places if you have not done so already. Both have free admission.

I would like to take this opportunity to thank the patient souls who read all or parts of this story and who offered advice and encouragement, especially the Atsokan crew. And of course, ten thousand thanks to all the good folks at the University of Minnesota Press, with a special *tusen takk* to Erik Anderson.

Margi Preus is the author of many books for young readers, including *Enchantment Lake* (Minnesota, 2015), *The Clue in the Trees* (Minnesota, 2017), and the Newbery Honor–winning, *New York Times*–bestselling *Heart of a Samurai*. Books in the Enchantment Lake series have been awarded the Midwest Book Award and the Midwest Booksellers Choice Award. At home in Duluth, Minnesota, Margi likes to hike, cross-country ski, paddle a canoe or kayak, or sit quietly with a book. She enjoys traveling and visiting schools all over the world.